MINI-MYSTERIES
by Julia Remine Piggin

SCHOLASTIC BOOK SERVICES
New York Toronto London Auckland Sydney Tokyo

ISBN: 0-590-04412-5

Copyright © 1973 by Scholastic Magazines, Inc. All rights reserved. Published by Scholastic Book Services, a division of Scholastic Magazines, Inc.

14 13   12   11   10   0 1 2 3 4 5/8

Printed in the U.S.A.

01

Contents

1 / LADY OUT
OF THE RAIN

Detective Inspector Bill Tawson was glad that a search for a rare book had taken him to the town's main library the day before. He'd recognized the librarian on duty as his old high school classmate Sara Hull. But she'd changed in twenty years from a mousy little girl into a vivid, intelligent-looking woman — "Yes, attractive," said Bill, surprised at his feelings after two years of widowerhood. Now the hazel eyes were sparkling with life and humor as Sara Hull faced Bill over coffee at the end of an excellent dinner in the dining room of the Crown Hotel.

"I've always thought I'd like to be a detective," Sara was saying, as a short man in a black suit rushed up to their table. "Oh, Inspector Tawson," he said in a breathless whisper, "I'm so glad you're here! There's been a murder in room 117.

I'm the night manager — it's Mrs. Bronwen de Pugh. She checked in last night — " The man was babbling as Bill leaped up and followed him out of the dining room. Sara hesitated.

"I know I shouldn't," she thought. Then, impulsively, she walked quickly after the two men, into the elevator, down the corridor to room 117, where a horrified chambermaid cowered in the tiny vestibule.

A young woman in a gray pantsuit lay sprawled across the bed, blood trickling from a bullet wound near the line of her flaming red hair. Bill grabbed the phone and called for an ambulance and officers, then began his official investigation. As he leaned over the woman's body, Sara looked around the room. In a corner stood a stack of expensive-looking pink suitcases, each stamped in gold with the initials B. de P. The closet door was open, and in it hung a half dozen costly outfits: a rose-pink chiffon gown, a fuschia wool coat, a scarlet suit, a white raincoat with a hood, a beige dress with a bright pink flowered scarf. "Did you see Miss de Pugh when she registered last night?" she asked the flustered manager.

"Oh, yes," he replied. "It was a rainy night and she was wearing one of those raincoats with a hood that hid half her face, but this is the luggage she brought, all right, and that's her purse on the dresser — I remember it." Bill checked the identification cards in the pocketbook — all were in the name of Bronwen de Pugh, but the wallet contained no cash.

Sara beckoned to him. "Bill, it's none of my

business," she said. "I know I shouldn't interfere, and I could be wrong. But I don't think the luggage and the clothes in the closet belong to that girl on the bed." She moved closer and spoke even more quietly.

Next day a package arrived at the library. In it was a handsome pin engraved with Sara's initials. Bill's card read: "You were right. We caught Bronwen de Pugh at the state line. She confessed. The girl had been blackmailing her. She figured leaving everything behind would make us think she, herself, was the dead woman, and give her a head start while we checked. Thanks, Ms. Sherlock Holmes — those initials are no coincidence."

What did Sara whisper to Bill?

"I don't think any woman with bright red hair ever traveled with an all pink and red wardrobe — not one thing in green or blue or brown, a redhead's most becoming colors."

2 / THE BOYS WHO DROPPED OUT

"Sara, have you heard of either Bob Sujet or Shandy Cumberbatch?"

Sara Hull nodded in answer to the Inspector's question.

"Yes, Bill, I do some volunteer work with high school dropouts, and I've met them both. Bob is one of those restless kids who's mad at the world and at himself. Not a bad student, but couldn't settle down to school — candidate for drug abuse, I'd be afraid. Shandy had a different problem, even more frustrating. He isn't really a dropout at all, for he's never been to school. Grew up in Appalachia, never had shoes to wear, and was too proud to go to school barefoot. I tried to persuade him that it wasn't too late, but he couldn't face the idea of going back now, so I'm afraid he may go through life illiterate. Angry about it too. Why?"

8

"Miss Rogers of the Star Employment Agency sent both boys over to the Riggs Office Building on Saturday afternoon. Nobody was around when they got there — there's a man on duty, but he says he never saw them, and the outside door was open. Self-service elevators, of course. Boys were supposed to report to Arnold Golman, of Golman Insurance, on the seventeenth floor, to move some machines. Golman was there alone. He told Miss Rogers to give the boys identification, and to tell them to knock and say who they were, and he'd unlock the door. Well, he was found dead, wallet and watch gone, head bashed in. Office rifled.

"We've talked to both boys. They're prime suspects, for Golman wouldn't have opened to just anybody. Bob says he went up in the elevator, knocked on the door and called, received no answer, got mad, and left. Time checks — it was after the lab says Golman was killed. Shandy admits he got there earlier, but says he only went as far as the lobby of the building, decided not to go up to the office. But he won't tell us why. He acts as if he's hiding something, Sara. Frankly, I suspect him."

"Mind if I call Miss Rogers?" Sara dialed the agency number, and asked the agent a question.

"Why, of course," Miss Rogers said. "That is, I told them the Golman Agency at the Riggs Building and wrote the rest on a slip of paper. What's that? Well, no, I don't think I did — but — " Sara hung up with thanks and gave Bill Miss Rogers' answer to her question.

9

"I guess that tells you which of the boys is a legitimate suspect, doesn't it?" she said, and the detective nodded.

What was the question Sara asked Miss Rogers?

"Did you tell the boys the office was on the seventeenth floor?" Miss Rogers hadn't, which ruled Shandy out. He couldn't read what she had written on the slip of paper, and couldn't read the room directory in the building lobby, as Bob could. So, not knowing where to go, he left.

3 / THE GALWAY GUITARS

THE GALWAY GUITARS
LEADING ROCK GROUP OF IRELAND
IN FIRST AMERICAN CONCERT AT EIGHT TONIGHT
AT THE CENTRAL BRANCH OF THE LIBRARY

The city seemed plastered with posters, and by six o'clock young people had started to gather to be sure of getting good seats. Sara Hull beamed. "It's a wonderful ad for the library."

But Detective Inspector Bill Tawson was all business. "We've had a tip that one of the Galway Guitars is from Galway, but can't even play a guitar," he confided to Sara. "According to our source, Wishy O'Mara, the young IRA leader, has slipped out of Ireland in place of one of the real singers. He's related to the boy and looks a lot like him — and the trouble is, he's played it so smart he's never been arrested, so there are no fingerprints. He's supposed to be planning to go to New York where the Guitars are scheduled to appear next, and plant a bomb in the British Embassy. We'd pick up all five of 'em, but one boy is the son of a diplomat and there's likely to be a sticky incident if we do. However, Officer Patner there—" he indicated a long-haired young man who looked like a confirmed hippie "—is a good guitar player on the side. He's going to watch carefully, and point out the guy who's faking — they say this Wishy doesn't know one end of a musical instrument from the other."

The Galway Guitars, however, had anticipated this police approach. They arrived at the library ruddy and cheerful — and all with heavily bandaged left hands. "We'll have a bit of a time accompanying ourselves tonight — we all got caught in the same swinging door," the leader explained as the audience roared with laughter. "However, our brave Irish voices will more than make up for our wee difficulty — a one-handed Irishman is as good as a three-handed Englishman, after all."

"Okay, Sherlock," Bill said to Sara after exchanging an exasperated glance with Patner. "Which one do you think it is? And if you don't know, how do you propose we find out?"

"Simple," said Sara. "Fingerprint them all."

"Sherlock, you're usually a good listener. I told you, we don't have O'Mara's prints — what would we compare them with?"

"Nothing," said Sara. "Now *you* listen." And, very quietly, she explained how fingerprinting the

12

Galway Guitars would trap the elusive Wishy O'Mara.

Two hours later, O'Mara was behind bars waiting for a deportation order. The other Guitars, blustering and ranting, but basically resigned at the thought of the thousands of dollars waiting for them, were on their way to New York with eight unbandaged hands.

What did Sara tell Bill?

A guitar player develops hard little pads at the ends of his fingers. The officer fingerprinting the group members was able to discover which one didn't have the pads — the one who couldn't be a professional guitarist.

4 / THE PICASSO THIEF

"Help! Help! Stop, thief! I've been robbed!"

Sara Hull dropped the dinner roll she was eating and rushed into the hall outside her apartment. Other doors opened, and neighbors came out to see Miss Nella Parsony rushing up and down the corridor, shouting and wringing her hands. Miss Parsony's graying hair was damp, and her bare ankles showed under a blue terry cloth bathrobe that showed damp stains. Sara ran to her.

"Please! Tell us what happened, Miss Parsony."

"Oh, it was horrible — that dreadful face! He took my Picasso — maybe other things, I haven't had time to check!" The neighbors gasped. Miss Parsony had invested a fortune in her art collection. "Oh, if only I hadn't left my bedroom window open. I never do, but this time — oh, his face! I was in the bathroom taking a hot shower — that's why I didn't hear him — had the door shut and the window too. I turned off the shower and stepped out and had just put on my robe — this one. I was standing at the basin, just about to brush my teeth, when the door was flung open and there he was! I was too terrified to turn around but I saw his face in the mirror! A big, red, crude face, and he grinned — he only had a few teeth, an awful smile — I thought he was going to kill me! And then he laughed and slammed the door so hard I couldn't get it open for a minute or two. When I got out I looked at the wall and my Picasso was gone. Oh, I'll have to see what else he took, I suppose — oh, somebody call the police." She collapsed hysterically in a heap on the bottom step of the stairs leading to the next floor.

"Sara, hadn't you better call your friend, that detective?" Mr. Smith looked concerned. "Maybe if we act right away, they could catch this man."

"Miss Parsony, come into my apartment, and we'll see what we can do," Sara said, taking the crying woman by the arm and steering her through the door. Inside, she pushed Miss Parsony into a chair. "Now, pull yourself together and tell me something. If you needed money, couldn't you have sold the painting? Or did you and your accomplice plan to do that, too, after you collected the insurance money?"

If she had just stepped out of a hot shower in a closed room, the mirror would have been steamed over. She couldn't have seen a man's reflection in it.

Why didn't Sara believe Miss Parsony?

5 . THE SLIPPERY BROTHER

"I knew my mother was still angry with me because I married Sam." Tears welled up in Barbara Clark's blue eyes. "But I never thought she'd make a will and not even — well, not leave me anything, not even mention me. She had so much, and she knew about the baby's hospital bills and the private school Sandy has to go to. My brother Dick, he's the oldest, says it's perfectly legal, even though she made it at home — it was properly witnessed and everything. The courthouse doesn't even send you a copy of a will if you're not mentioned in it. I just yelled at Dick on the phone until he sent me one — I think he and I have been yelling at each other all our lives."

Barbara dug into her bag and handed Sara Hull a smeary copy of a handwritten document. "Look at it — how could she do it, Sara?"

17

The will read:

"To my son, Richard, I leave the art collection amassed by my late husband.

"To my older daughter, Althea, I leave all my jewelry, except for my emerald ring, which I leave to my granddaughter, Anne, daughter of my son Charles.

"To my son Charles, I leave the furnishings of my two homes, in Crown Point and Newport, R. I.

"To each of my faithful servants I leave the sum of five thousand dollars.

"And to all my beloved children, I leave the sum of one million dollars, to be divided equally among them.

"The residue of my estate . . ."

Sara looked up, puzzled. "Why, Barbara," she said, "you are mentioned. Your mother left you a very substantial legacy. Don't you see? If I had a brother like Dick, I'd yell at him, too, for not sending me a copy of the will."

What did Sara mean?

The will refers to "my older daughter, Althea," then goes on to say, ". . . to all my beloved children." Barbara's mother was obviously acknowledging the fact that she also had a younger daughter, who had to be included among her children.

6 / SHERLOCK HOLMES REINCARNATED?

"I'll miss you, Owen," Sara said as she handed her young assistant his final paycheck. "And I'm sorry you're not going on to college. But I guess finding yourself is important too. Maybe later."

"Oh, I'm not dropping out to find myself," Owen laughed. "I've already found myself. That's the reason I'm getting a full-time job — so I can pay for classes with Gandalfa at night until I uncover all the knowledge inside me. You see, Gandalfa has the gift of telling you who you were in a past life. He can do that right away, just by watching you for half an hour or so. But after that he knows how to guide you to all the hidden talent and know-how, and, well, like everything that maybe made you a big wheel in some other time. I guess I shouldn't tell you, but I was Henry Ford. And I still really know how to invent stuff, and make money, and all. I just have to be able to get in touch with it. After I've gone to Gandalfa for a while, it'll only be a couple of years before I'm just as rich and important as I was before!"

"Oh, no, Owen," Sara protested. "Even if you *could* find out for sure who you were in a previous incarnation, the knowledge wouldn't be given to you to make you rich and famous. It would be given to help you grow spiritually — everything I've ever studied about rebirth teaches that. Owen, this Gandalfa — "

"He knows his stuff, Miss Hull! He did it with you! He didn't know anything about you at all — nothing about how you can solve mysteries and all. And he came into the library one day and sat over there and watched you. And he knew right away. He said, 'That woman is the reincarnation of the great detective Sherlock Holmes.' See? How could he come up with that? That's why you're so good at figuring things out. You did it before. You were the greatest!"

Sara looked amazed. "Owen," she said. "Don't you realize you've just proved that Gandalfa is nothing but a money-hungry fake? I don't know who I may have been in an earlier life — but I *know* it wasn't Sherlock Holmes!"

Could Sara really know?

Yes. Sherlock Holmes never lived — he was invented by Sir Arthur Conan Doyle.

20

7 / BETTY'S COUSIN

"What, taking out books on American history? And on Saturday morning? I thought Central High's most famous actress would sleep till noon on weekends!"

Betty Goldstein laughed at Sara Hull's teasing.

"They're not for me, they're for my cousin Esther. Maybe you read the story about her in the paper — she's from Israel, spending the summer here. I dropped by to see her this morning, and she was saying she wanted to know all about America, so I thought I'd take these books over to her tomorrow."

"She's not staying with your family?"

"Oh, no. She was supposed to, and then she found out that we weren't Orthodox Jews. She's very strict and religious, and she moved to a rooming house where they serve kosher meals and all that."

21

Betty turned to leave, almost colliding at the library door with a slim, sandy-haired young man who stopped and called her by name. In the library quiet, Sara could pick up most of what he said.

"Your cousin Esther . . . she said you might be here . . . walking on the street, mugger grabbed her purse, knocked her down . . . I live near there . . . all upset . . . I'll drive you over if you like . . ."

"Yes, of course . . ."

Sara's voice was sharp as she called, "Betty, come over here! You didn't fill out these request slips properly — come back and do it right!"

Startled, with a "Be right back" to the young man, Betty ran to the far end of the long, hollow-oval library desk, where Sara was waving a blank request slip. "Miss Hull, I don't understand. I've got to go to my cousin — she's been hurt —"

"Betty," Sara said, "nothing has happened to your cousin. That young man is lying. Now, you're an actress — start a loud argument with me over these request slips to drown me out while I call the police."

Later, Bill Tawson patted Sara's shoulder admiringly.

"Sherlock," he said, "I say it again. I wish I had you on my detective squad. You probably saved that girl's life. That guy is wanted for questioning in three rape-murder cases — got pretty girls like Betty to get in his car on some pretext and then — but there's one thing I don't understand.

Why were you so positive Esther Goldstein hadn't been mugged?"

What was Sara's answer?

"Esther is an Orthodox Jew — and no Orthodox Jewish woman carries a pocketbook on the Sabbath."

8 / WINNIE-THE-POOH, SKYJACKER

Stewardesses moved up and down the narrow aisles of the jetliner, collecting the last of the dinner trays. Sara Hull leaned back in her seat, hoping to nap a little before the plane landed in another hour. She was hardly aware of the tall, dark-haired man who stood up, pushed his way past the nearest stewardess, and held up two stuffed Winnie-the-Pooh bears.

"Your attention, ladies and gentlemen," he said, smiling triumphantly. "As those nearest to me can see, each of these little Pooh bears has been cut open and sewn up again. In one there is only what all true and authentic Pooh bears should contain — a candy heart that reads 'I love you.' Remember that from your childhood? But in the other, there is also a little device I have placed, a little device that the unscientific among you would

24

probably call a bomb. It is very sensitive. If I drop it at just a certain angle, an angle that I know very well, it will go off and all of us will go to our reward. However, if you prefer, only I will receive a reward. Young lady — " he half turned to the stewardess " — please go into the pilot's cabin and tell the captain what I have just told all these good people. Tell him I want the plane to put down in London, where I will be provided with a parachute and three hundred thousand dollars in cash — unmarked, of course. I'm not greedy. I could ask for more, couldn't I? When I have my supplies, the passengers can leave the plane. The pilot and one of you pretty stewardesses will stay with me until we find a suitable spot over Italy, where I will leave you — after setting Winnie-the-Pooh down very, very carefully. And tell that husky young copilot not to try to jump me from behind — Pooh Bear will drop at the touch of a hat, to coin a phrase. Go on, now, dear. And you — " he beckoned to another stewardess " — come up and stand close to me while your friend is gone."

The second stewardess moved forward. As she passed Sara Hull's seat, the librarian pulled at her sleeve.

"It's a hoax," she told the girl in a low tone. "Tell the captain this as soon as you can — it's his decision, but I'm sure there's no bomb in that Pooh Bear." She continued whispering in the stewardesses's ear.

The stewardess didn't get a chance to tell the captain until the plane had put down in London

25

and the passengers were allowed to file off, while the skyjacker, bear still in hand, counted green bills in a suitcase with the other hand. But then the captain took his chance. He grabbed the bear from the skyjacker's hand and hurled it through the open door of the aircraft, into an area the police had cleared of people. It bounced harmlessly on the ground, as Scotland Yard men closed in.

Sara Hull stood in the airport lounge as the plane's crew appeared, and the captain kissed her in front of a TV camera and the world. "I wouldn't have had the nerve," he said, "if what you told the stewardess hadn't made me remember my little sister."

What did Sara tell the stewardess?

"He's lying, if he really had opened up that bear, he couldn't have seen a candy heart. It was Raggedy Ann, not Winnie-the-Pooh, who had a candy heart sewn inside her."

9 / THE CONFESSION OF BARRYMORE YORICK

"Sara Hull, I have a confession to make — to the press." Barrymore Yorick's white head was held high. "This morning's paper says that Edmond Edgerton is near death at the Old Actors' Home. Before he dies, I must clear his name — and only I can do so."

Sara looked puzzled. "Edmond Edgerton — the silent film star?" she said. "He was accused of murdering his wife, wasn't he? But he was acquitted, as I remember. I don't understand."

"How could you?" Yorick made a dramatic gesture. "Let me speak. Then you *will* understand. And, I trust, help me to purge my conscience.

"In 1920 Babette Lamere was the most beautiful and adored actress of the silver screen. Edward Edgerton was her husband, her great romance — but not her equal in fame. One dawn, after a night of partying alone, Edgerton returned to the London hotel suite he shared with his wife, and found her — he said — strangled with a scarf. No one had seen an intruder. There was no sign of robbery or forced entry. Edgerton himself was accused and tried. Professional jealousy, the prosecutor cried. But evidence was too slight. He was acquitted, as you say. But not by the public who had loved Babette. His career waned, and now he is dying, old, poor, still in the shadow of doubt and disgrace.

"I could lift it. I could, perhaps, have saved him from it. You see, in 1920 — more than fifty years ago — I was an aspiring but impoverished young actor in London. On the afternoon of the murder I was walking in a little park near the Edgertons' hotel, looking up at the windows, wishing I might meet them in the flesh — I had seen them only on the screen. Suddenly, from an isolated bench, I heard a woman's voice — a voice I knew, the unmistakable, gentle, lisping, innocent voice of a thousand roles — the famous voice of Babette Lamere. And it was pleading, 'No, no, spare my marriage, my dearest husband — spare my career. I will pay you what you ask.' A coarse, rough, unfamiliar male voice replied, 'That's sensible of you. I'll come to your hotel room tonight at about eleven. Get rid of Eddie — tell him you've got a headache — he can go out alone. And remember — if you don't fork over the full amount, I go to the papers with a bit of information, and the proof I won't give you without the money.'

28

"Miss Hull, I was thunderstruck. But what could I do? I watched the blackmailer leave the park from one direction, the lovely girl of my dreams walk slowly away in the other. That night I guess she thought better of buying whatever vileness he had to sell, and, in a rage, he strangled her. At least I could have told Scotland Yard that she was expecting someone that night so that suspicion would not have fallen upon poor Edgerton alone. But I was afraid for my own safety, if the evil blackmailer knew of my presence in the park. I remained silent. But now, long overdue though it is — "

"Mr. Yorick, please," Sara Hull interrupted. "I know you'd like some publicity — it might help get you a character part or two, or you might even be paid for this story now that film libraries are showing Babette Lamere films again. But your memory can't be as good as it was when you played Iago. You've forgotten something — your story can't be true."

What did Yorick forget?

Something pretty obvious. In 1920 motion pictures were silent. He couldn't have recognized Babette's voice from seeing her films.

29

10 / THE PHONY SCOT

Sara Hull and Bill Tawson had discovered they both had a few Scottish ancestors. To honor them, and because they both thrilled to bagpipe music, the librarian and the detective inspector were spending the day at the annual Highland Games being held this holiday weekend in a field outside town.

After watching brawny men toss the tree trunk called the caber, eating hot meat pies, and watching spirited Highland dancing, Sara and Bill joined the crowd swarming around the bandstand where bagpipe competitions were being held. Sara drank in the wild music, sighed deeply, and said, "You know, I think I'm developing an Aberdeen accent."

A tall, dark man who looked like a clan chief frowned down at her. He wore a bright, swinging kilt and touched the band on his Glengarry bonnet as he told her, "Ye should be wearin' a dress, or at least a scarf of your clan plaid, lassie." He spoke with an exaggerated rolling of the r's. "A good Scotchwoman like you should be showin' it," he finished, and with mock, or perhaps real, contempt he shouldered his way through the crowd in the direction of the bandstand.

Sara shook her head. "You know, Bill," she began, "for a man who wears a kilt and a Glengarry, that man — " She was interrupted by a scream higher and more plaintive than any note of the pipes. Bill grabbed her arm and pulled her after him through the press of people, toward the sound. A man lay on his side near the bandstand, blood as bright as his kilt spreading around a wound in his back. A *skean dhu*, the sharp Highland dagger, lay on the ground, and a woman in a blouse that matched the kilt knelt beside him.

"Oh, Angus," she wailed, "they said they'd kill you, and they have, they have."

"Who said that?" Bill Tawson held out his police credentials, as Games officials ran to call an ambulance and summon more police.

"The racketeers — we have a wee store and he wouldn't pay for protection. He told them he was a Scot and a Scot took care of himself. They said they'd show all the Scots in the neighborhood. That's why they did it here — " she broke into sobs.

Sara Hull glanced sharply about her, then cried out with urgent authority. "There!" She pointed to the edge of the crowd, where the tall man who had chided her was turning to walk away. "That man! Grab him, somebody!" The man started to run, but three big caber-tossers caught up with him and pinned his arms.

"There's blood on his hands!" one of them shouted. They dragged him, struggling and protesting — in a voice minus a Scottish burr — toward Bill, who stood with his gun drawn. Heads swiveled in Sara's direction.

"How did you know, lass?" asked a man in a dark Douglas jacket. "Of all the men here, how could you pick out that one? We were closer than you and we didn't see him use the dagger."

"I didn't see it either," Sara said. "But he came from that direction. And whatever he was, I knew he was only pretending to be a Scot."

How did Sara know?

The material out of which kilts are made is called tartan by Scots, not plaid. A plaid is a garment worn over the shoulder. And, Scots refer to themselves as that — not Scotchmen or Scotchwomen.

11 / A WALK
IN THE PARK

"I wonder if the father of our country ever spent his own birthday the way we're celebrating it, tramping through the snow in a park."

Sara Hull laughed, her breath misting in the winter air. "You've got to admit black branches and blue sky and white snow are beautiful," she said. "I'm glad that for once you got a day off on the same day the library was closed, Bill."

Around a bend in the park path a heavily bundled figure came rushing toward Bill and Sara. It was Clement Barber, owner of the town's largest factory.

"Bill Tawson," the man exclaimed. "What a break! I guess you have the day off, too, but I wish you'd come with me, just for friendship's sake. I'm on my way to see my brother — you know, he lives in that apartment house overlooking the park. This morning — about half an hour ago — he called me and said he'd just received a threatening letter in the mail, and wanted to see me about it. Something about the action he's trying to take in the town council on air pollution. I didn't want to call the police until I'd found out what it was all about — but now that I've met you, Inspector — "

Ten minutes later, admitted by the apartment superintendent after no one had answered Barber's bell, Bill, Sara, and Clement were bending over the bleeding body of Robert Barber, who had been beaten repeatedly with a heavy brass book-end that lay beside him.

"But where's the letter you say he got?" Bill asked, after phoning for an ambulance.

"The rat who did this must have taken it to cover his tracks!" Clement paced the floor, wringing his hands. "I should have come sooner — I didn't realize — "

Sara stepped in front of him, looked him squarely in the face.

"It would have been hard to get back here much sooner," she said. "Your factory has been cited for polluting the air, hasn't it? An incident like this would be quite a warning for other members of the council, wouldn't it? You see, Mr. Bar-

34

ber, your story can't be true. Your brother didn't call and say he'd just received a threatening letter."

What did Sara mean?

Washington's Birthday is a national holiday, on which there is no mail delivery.

12 / THE STATUE
OF ST. ELIZABETH

Light filtered through the blue and gold stained-glass window above the pulpit, giving the Rev. Dr. Stinwell a multicolored robe as he smiled benignly down on his congregation.

"We have had a rare and blessed offer," the pastor announced. "A visitor to this church, who wishes to remain anonymous, has acquired, in his extensive travels, a holy object. It is a small statue of Elizabeth, mother of John the Baptist, cousin of the Virgin Mary. But this is not just another statue. It is contemporary — I mean, it was carved from life by a village sculptor who knew Elizabeth in the years before either John or Jesus was born. Yes, I can hear your unspoken comment. It *is* costly. But when we think that Our Lord Himself may have touched it in his cousin's home, I am sure the members of our vestry will be anxious to acquire it."

After the service Sara Hull slipped into the sacristy, where Dr. Stinwell was hanging up his now plain white robe. "Doctor Stinwell," she said, "may I ask a question? Why are you so convinced that the statue of Elizabeth was really carved from life?"

"Why, my dear, it says so! The sculptor carved both her name and his and the date on the base. Oh, the stone has been carbon tested to prove its age. And, not only that, but I took a photograph of it and showed it to a seminary classmate of mine who happens to be one of the leading Aramaic scholars in our church — Jesus and his family spoke Aramaic, you know. He confirmed what it said: 'Elizabeth, woman of Juda, wife of Zechariah, carved by Isaac, son of Seth, her friend, in the year 3 B.C.'"

"Oh, Dr. Stinwell." Sara touched the elderly clergyman's hand. "You and your friend are both too trusting. I'm sure the statue is very old. And I'm sure the translation of the inscription is correct. But don't you see? It couldn't possibly be authentic."

Why couldn't it?

Three years before anyone even knew Jesus was to be born, no one could possibly have dated anything B.C.—"Before Christ."

13 / THE GIRL
WHO SCREAMED

Except for the silver flash of a great jet plane as it took off from the nearby airport, the treelined street could have belonged in an earlier, more peaceful America. Yet Sara Hull shuddered even as she stopped at the low steps of a neat white house and called over the engine noise, "Hello, Mrs. Gordon!"

"Why, Miss Hull," the old woman in the porch rocker shouted back. Then, more softly, as the plane winged away and Sara settled into a companion rocking chair, "What brings you way out here?"

"I've brought the book you had on reserve," Sara explained, holding out a novel in a bright dust jacket. "But, I guess you realize I wanted to talk to you too." Again a cold chill shivered up her spine as she thought of the terrible night a week before when a young girl, tenant in Mrs. Gordon's upstairs apartment, had been murdered in the yard behind the house. Almost as shattering, Glen Roper, one of Sara's young assistants, had been accused of the crime. Sara believed Glen's story: He had been waiting for a friend who lived across the street, and had seen the girl go down the narrow alley into the backyard, where outside stairs led to her apartment. A few seconds later, a rough-looking man had followed her. Glen had called out, "Watch out, miss!" Then he had heard a piercing scream. Leaping out of his car, he had rushed into the yard in time to see the man escaping over the fence. He had been bending over the girl, lying in a pool of blood, when a policeman who had also heard the scream came to investigate. By then the murderer was gone, and Glen was the only logical suspect. His one witness was Mrs. Gordon, who had been sitting on her porch, just as she was now, on the night of the murder. But she had refused to verify that he had not rushed past her until *after* her tenant's scream.

"Mrs. Gordon," Sara began hopefully, "Glen is a fine boy. Are you sure—"

"Of course I'm sure," Mrs. Gordon snapped, her eyes glittering. "Fine, fiddlesticks. None of them are fine, with their long hair—that girl, one man after another. That's why I didn't notice who went back there after her. And as far as that scream they talk about goes—I didn't hear it. I'm deaf. Right now, I'm talking to you because

I'm reading your lips. Couldn't have heard a scream. I told the police, and I'll go to court — "

"And so will I," said Sara Hull. "You don't like young people, Mrs. Gordon, but that's no reason to tell a lie that can ruin Glen's life. I'll testify that I know you're lying."

How did Sara know?

If Mrs. Gordon had really been deaf, she wouldn't have shouted over the plane's engine noise, then lowered her voice when it was gone.

14 / THE CARROLL MANUSCRIPT

"I'm Herbert Carroll, Miss Hull." The Englishman shook Sara's hand and sat down in the chair beside her desk. "I know that the rare book collection of this library is relatively small. But the great libraries of the world have so many priceless manuscripts that I've decided to make this one available to a library in which it will be more of a treasure."

Sara glanced at the black case Mr. Carroll balanced on his knee. She was interested. "What is the manuscript?" she asked. With a dramatic gesture, the man produced a worn old notebook. "This has been in the Carroll family for more than a hundred years. It is one of the workbooks of my great-uncle, Lewis Carroll. As you of course know, the famous author of *Alice in Wonderland* never married. But his possessions were preserved by the Carrolls who came after him, and this was left to me. I hate to part with it, but — finances — "

Sara took the shabby book and turned the brittle pages with awe and care. She knew it was genuine. She had studied Lewis Carroll's handwriting at the British Museum when preparing a term paper in her college days, and the script was unmistakable.

"Mr. Carroll," she said, "this is a rare opportunity for us. As it happens, the chairman of the library committee is in the reference room upstairs. He's a bit deaf — can't use the phone very well — so if you'll wait I'll run up and get him. I want him to see this wonderful notebook — before you change your mind."

Sara rushed upstairs, but not to the reference room — to a telephone. To her friend Bill Tawson she said, "Do the police have anything on a theft from a museum or library — England or America? An original Lewis Carroll notebook? A man is here offering to sell one, and I know it's real. But I also know he's lying about where he got it. Yes? I thought so. I'll stall him until you can get here."

What gave Mr. Carroll away?

The name Lewis Carroll was a pen name, derived form the author's two *given* names. Relatives would have been named Dodgson, his real last name.

15 / NOTE TO AN UNKNOWN WOMAN

"Miss Hull, have you seen the paper?" The tall boys in blue jeans thrust a copy of *The Gazette* across the library desk. "Arch Vanderhorn's been kidnapped! We knew you'd want to know right away, since you were such a good friend of his."

Sara Hull took the paper and read the headline: VANDERHORN HEIR ABDUCTED. There was a photograph of Arch's gentle, sensitive face, and another of the peculiar note found in his room and the envelope in which it had been contained. The letter had been painstakingly pieced together with words and letters, some capitals, some small, cut from newspapers and magazines. But the address on the envelope and the signature were in Arch Vanderhorn's familiar handwriting: *For Roselle McKhosh*, the address read.

As Sara held the paper up to the light for a closer look, blown-up prints of the same photographs were pushed under her nose. Bill Tawson's voice said, "Here. These ought to be easier to read."

Sara looked up at her friend, the detective inspector, and smiled in spite of her concern for Arch. She had sometimes thought she was the only friend the lonely boy had made since he had graduated from the expensive prep school his always-traveling parents had chosen. His only interest had seemed to be word games — anagrams, puzzles of all kinds, and she had enjoyed recommending books about them to him.

"Is this really how it happened, Bill?" she asked, scanning the newspaper account.

"Yes, the bedroom was ripped apart as if the boy had fought like a tiger," Bill said. "Of course, the parents were in Europe — they're flying back — and the servants sleep in another part of the house, so nobody heard anything. Must have been carefully planned — that note took a while to put together. But the mystery is — not why they forced the kid to address it — but who is Roselle McKhosh? The butler's been there 25 years, and says they've never had a servant named that. I think the kid was trying to tell us something, but what?"

Again Sara examined the picture of the pasted letters:

no polIce or they May FINish mE. JUST
WAit uNTil thEy Dial you. They will sOon,
So pleAse none of Your FAncy tRickEry.

44

WhEre they'LL take me, i don't know, but if
you LOVE me, wait. ARCH.

The librarian laughed aloud. Bill Tawson and
the two teenagers looked at her in amazement as
she said, "You brought it to the right place. This
note is addressed to me."

"To you?" the three chorused.

"Yes, to me." Sara looked at her watch. "If
this was found last night, I'm sure it's all right to
tell you. Arch must be wherever he's going by
now. He hasn't been kidnapped. He staged this
whole thing himself, to stir up those parents of
his — it'll be the first time they've given him a
thought in the last year, I'd be willing to bet. He
knows they'll find him, but this way he thought
he might have a little time away from that cold,
lonely house to think things out and enjoy some
freedom. But he wanted to tell me good-bye, so
he did it with the things he likes best: an anagram, and a very simple puzzle. Come on, Bill
Tawson — do you think you're the only person
who realizes that SH stands for both Sara Hull
and Sherlock Holmes?"

What did Sara Mean?

farewell. Love, Arch.
in Arch's note, it says: I'm fine. Just wanted to say
Holmes. And if you read only the capital letters
scramble the letters and you'll have — Sherlock
The name Roselle McKhosh is an anagram. Un-

45

16 / THE PET SHOP
RIP-OFF

"Let's see if there are any puppies in the pet shop window," Sara said to Bill Tawson. "Poor Mr. Gray hasn't been doing so well, but there might be some. This isn't a very good location."

They crossed the quiet street, but there was no quiet inside the little shop. Through the shop window they could see two teenaged boys struggling fiercely with each other, and Mr. Gray slumped unconscious over the counter.

Drawing his gun, Bill surged through the door and the boys fell apart.

As Sara called an ambulance, one boy cried, "It was him! He was trying to rob the cash register and I jumped him!"

"You lie!" yelled the other boy. "I caught you!"

"I know both these boys," Sara said after completing her call. "George Simmons and Hal Ferrell. They both worked for Mr. Gray up until about three months ago, when his business began to get so bad. I can't believe either one of them would do this. How did you both happen to be here today?"

"I've been coming in to teach the myna birds to talk," George answered. "You can check, one of them says 'Hi, George.' People like them to be able to say something when they buy them. Of course, they just pick some things up — "

"I came to see if the baby rabbits had been born yet," Hal said, glaring at George. "Some were expected when I left, and Mr. Gray said I could have one."

"Oh, now, come on," George began, making a move toward Hal. Bill stiffened, and Sara shook her head.

"No more trouble please," she said. "I know who the thief is, and which one is the hero, and I think both these boys know that I do."

Which one was it?

Hal. The gestation period of rabbits is 31 days. Both boys knew that if they'd been expected three months before, they'd hardly be "babies" now.

17 / THE PRODIGAL HEIR

Zerelda Stevenson had never married, but stayed at home and cared for her scholarly, aged father who seemed to live to see that etiquette was observed and things were done "properly." At least, everyone thought, she would inherit his money and property and be able to enjoy life after he died. The old gentleman's son and namesake, Lance, had left home at 17 and never even corresponded with his family. But Lance had turned up for his father's funeral, and not just to pay his final respects. In his pocket was a will, dated after the will found in old Lance's safe deposit box which left everything to Zerelda. His father had mailed the new will to him, young Lance ex-

48

claimed. It was properly drawn up and witnessed. And, except for a few pieces of silver and jewelry left to Zerelda, it named Lance as his father's heir.

Calling a few days after the funeral, Sara Hull found Zerelda packing a trunk, her eyes red from crying, but her head held high. "Yes, I'm hurt and angry," she admitted, "but I won't let it get me down. There must be some kind of job I can find. I'll go away and — "

"Before you make definite plans," Sara said, "could I see a copy of that will? I assume Lance gave you one." "It's right here," Zerelda said, reaching into the trunk and producing a folded document.

Sara opened it and began to read: "I, Lance Stevenson I, being of sound mind — " She ran her eyes down the page. Just as she had heard, it left almost everything to "my beloved son, Lance Stevenson II." The signature was in the same handwriting in which old Lance had signed his library card. Sara laughed out loud.

"You think it's *funny?*" Zerelda blazed.

"Funny that an intelligent woman like you ever supposed for one minute that this ridiculous forgery was genuine," Sara told her. "Really, Zerelda, I'm surprised at you. Stop that packing right now and call your brother Lance — and you might consider calling the police too."

What was wrong with the will?

Men who are the first to bear a name don't sign themselves "John Smith I" but just "John Smith." And a son named for his father is called "John Smith Jr." not "John Smith II" — that's used by another relative named for the first John Smith.

18 / THE MAN AT THE BELLE FONTAINE

Usually Sara Hull could tune out sounds, but the voice of the young man using the phone booth about ten feet away from her desk broke through her mental barrier. For one thing, the door was half open. He couldn't fit the long narrow package he carried into the booth and still shut the folding door.

"Okay, okay," he was saying, "I get it, I said okay. If it rains, it won't be open so I won't try it. No, I don't know where I'll be. There's gotta be a motel around — I'll ask somebody. Gotta live cheap until the payoff." He hung up, struggled out of the booth with his package, and started toward the library desk. Something about the shape of the package and his arrogant manner triggered a vague, painful memory for Sara, a sense of shock and sadness. "What is it?" she asked herself, and then the memory flooded in, agonizingly clear.

51

"You know of any cheap place around here I could stay?" The sharp voice interrupted her train of thought.

The words the man had spoken in the booth flashed into Sara's mind. "Yes," she said, "I do know one. The Belle Fontaine Motel — just a few miles out along Route 6. It's inexpensive and clean."

"That'll do." Hoisting his burden, the young man sauntered out, as Sara picked up the phone, dialed, and spoke hurriedly.

"Max, this is Sara Hull. Fine — listen, please. A man carrying a long narrow package is coming out there for a room. Give him one on the courtyard, and make the price so low he couldn't consider leaving. He *must* stay there tonight. It's important." She lowered her voice, added a few more words, then, "Please. I'll alert Bill Tawson. And be sure to give him plenty of water in the morning."

Next day the sun shone brightly on a city colorful with flags and bunting. Crowds began to line the streets early in the day to watch the President's limousine pass on the way to an election rally. The President stood in the back of his open car, smiling and waving. The evening papers and TV reports commented happily on the lack of violence. But over after-dinner coffee in Sara's apartment, Bill Tawson wiped his brow for the twentieth time.

"Sherlock," he said, "I don't understand it. We had the place staked out all morning, but the guy never came out until more than an hour after the Presidential motorcade went through town. You were right about that package — there *was* a gun in it, unregistered. We got him on that, and a concealed weapon charge, and they're checking his record. But what was funny — he came out wearing a raincoat and carrying an umbrella in his other hand. On a sunny day like today! The officers said he looked scared to death when he looked up at the sky — as if he couldn't believe it. Enlighten me."

"I just took a chance," Sara said, "that he wouldn't open the venetian blinds when he woke up in the morning."

And what did that mean?

Belle Fontaine, in French, means beautiful fountain. The motel had a fountain in the courtyard, and to anyone inside, the splashing of water sounded like rain. When the guest awoke, he thought it was raining — and that the President would have to ride in a closed car. Nobody could ever be sure, but Sara may have saved the country another assassination — because the young man with the long package reminded her of Lee Harvey Oswald, who shot President John F. Kennedy.

53

19 / THE WORRIED SON

"Sara, do you believe in premonitions?" Ambrose Wrye, the middle-aged art librarian, looked worried. "For days I've had a feeling that something has happened to my mother. Oh, I know, I haven't seen or spoken to her since she kicked me out for wanting to be a painter — that was 25 years ago. But this thing nags at me so, I even tried to call her this morning. But her number is unlisted and I can't get it. Sara, it's nearly lunchtime. Would you ride over there with me? I honestly couldn't face her alone after all these years. But she is my mother, and if she's in trouble — "

On the way to the Wrye house, Ambrose reminisced. "She was a pretty woman, always kept a dog, and made it clear it was hers, though she let me play with him. Knew a lot about art, but looked down on painters. Oh, well. Here we are."

Repeated doorbell ringing and knocking brought no response from inside the big old house. Walking around it, Ambrose and Sara could see nothing through the drawn window shades. Then Sara noticed that the back door was open a few inches. Ambrose bounded up the steps, held the door open so Sara could precede him into a dark little shed. She took a step, felt something cold and wet splash on her foot. "What is it?" Ambrose cried at her exclamation, lighting a match. Then they both relaxed. "Of course, you knocked over her puppy's water dish," he said. "I told you, she always kept a dog, and I guess she still does."

They moved into the kitchen, and this time Sara cried out as she bumped into someone heading toward the door. Hastily, Ambrose lit another match, and the face of a frightened teenage boy seemed to flicker in the light. "I didn't do it," the boy half sobbed. "I swear I didn't. I saw the door open — okay, I was going to take something, but she was dead when I got here!" He lunged past Ambrose and Sara, out through the shed into the yard.

"He doesn't matter!" Sara said. "Come on! The police will catch him! Get to your mother!"

In the lighted living room, an elderly woman lay on the floor. A tiny puppy crouched nearby, whining piteously. "Mother!" Ambrose screamed. But Mrs. Wrye had been beyond hearing for hours.

Sara went back into the kitchen, found the wall telephone, dialed Bill Tawson, the detective inspector. "Bill," she said, "Mrs. Wrye, Ambrose

Wrye's mother, is dead. She may have died of a stroke, she may have been killed by a teenaged prowler. But I think she was killed by her son."

Why did Sara think Ambrose killed his mother?

If Ambrose hadn't seen or been near his mother for 25 years, how did he know she had a puppy, not a full-grown dog?

20 / THE WISE OLD INDIAN

It wasn't often that a celebrity like Chief Blue Cloud came to town, and Mrs. Poemore, President of the local Literary Society, was dithering as she introduced him.

"Any of you who have copies of the Chief's wonderful biography, *Book of Blue Cloud*," she announced, beaming, "do come up and meet the Chief and have him autograph it." Soon the Chief was surrounded by people pressing books on him and dictating effusive messages for him to inscribe.

Half an hour later, as the strong punch took effect, the Chief sat alone, apparently forgotten, at the end of the room, looking wistfully at the admirers who chattered to their friends. Sara Hull pushed her way through the crowd and sat down beside him.

"I enjoyed your book, Chief Blue Cloud," she said. "You're 102 years old, I understand?"

"Yes, 102," the Chief nodded. "I know I don't look it, but the red man spends his youth in the air, under the sun and the trees, communicating with his brothers, the animals, and finds peace inside himself. So he does not age as the paleface does." The old man leaned toward Sara. "You know what this party reminds me of?" he said. "One night, long ago, I was rolled in a blanket, asleep on the prairie. I woke to find three pairs of burning eyes staring at me. Why they hadn't pounced on me I'll never know — the Great Spirit must have held them back. They were wolves, you see — a wolf and his two mates. I lay still, calling on my strong medicine, thinking of them as a brother and two sisters and trying to reach their minds. I don't know whether or not my mind touched theirs, but the wolf and his wives turned and trotted away. When these people devoured me for awhile with their hungry eyes, and then turned from me, I remembered that night."

Sara reached over and patted the old man's hand.

"Chief Blue Cloud," she said, raising her punch glass in a toast, "I congratulate you. Whether you're 102 or not, you've really put it over, haven't you? I liked your book — even though I had a feeling when I was reading it that most of your stories were made up out of whole cloth. I won't tell anybody — but I don't think you know as much about life on the prairie as I do."

How did Sara guess?

No wolf has two mates at the same time. Wolves take one mate, for life, as any Indian who lived in the wild would know.

21 / THE MURDERED HOSTESS

"Cheers!" Bill Tawson and Sara Hull raised their mugs of hot buttered rum as their host lifted his own mug to his lips. "Awfully glad you stopped by with the lady, Bill — nice to see an old friend the night before taking off on a vacation." Zeke Blalock's face looked ruddy in the light from the fireplace.

"I think we're imposing on you," Sara said. "I'd like to sit here in front of this open fire for hours, but you need to go up there and help your wife with the packing. Where did you say you were going?"

"Argentina," Zeke answered. "Listen, Agnes will be furious if I let you two get away without telling her you dropped in, packing or no packing. Let me run up and fetch her down." He set down his mug and bounded up the stairs. A moment later, they heard a roar, as if Zeke were in pain. Rushing up, they met him in the second-floor hall, his face contorted, his eyes wild.

"She's been killed! She's dead! My Agnes — down there, in our bedroom! I went in and she was slumped over the suitcase with a knife sticking out of her back! The window was open, the room was icy cold —" Bill and Sara were already on their way to the bedroom, where the scene was just as Zeke described it. Agnes had fallen across the case she was packing, her hands clinging to a heavy tweed suit, half in and half out of the suitcase. On the bed lay a plaid wool shirt and a pair of knitted socks, apparently waiting their turn to be packed.

"He must have broken in while we were down there toasting — the trip —" Zeke's voice wavered. Bill went to the window. "Too bad there's no snow," he said. "There'd be footprints. Look, I'd better make a call. The phone's in the hall, isn't it?" Zeke nodded, and Sara followed Bill out of the room.

"Oh, Bill, and he's a friend of yours," she said sadly. "He must have done it before we dropped in — we stopped him from escaping."

Why was Sara so sure?

Winter in the United States is summer in Argentina. Agnes wouldn't have been packing winter clothes for Zeke.

61

22 / THE CIVIL WAR AUCTION

"It's a good thing I'm not a male chauvinist," Bill Tawson said, looking fondly at Sara Hull. "A girl who knows as much as you do about as many things as you do, Sherlock, would really scare me off. Now, the Civil War, for example. You know a lot about that, don't you?"

"I do indeed," said Ms. Sara Hull. "And what does the detective bureau of our fair city need to know about the War Between the States?"

"Well, we've had a tip that the Star of Sharaze, one of the largest diamonds in the world — and, as you know, stolen from the famous actress who owned it back in September — is going to be auctioned off with some Civil War memorabilia this afternoon. It's hidden somewhere in one of the antiques — not a real antique, a phony that's been added to the collection just for the benefit of the receiver of stolen goods. We think the auctioneer is in on it, so we want to play it cool. Most of the Civil War buffs who go to these auctions are pretty knowledgeable and wouldn't be likely to bid on something that looked phony — but nobody on our staff is that much into the War. A hundred or so items are going to be auctioned and if we followed everybody who bought something — well —"

"So you want me to go to the auction and see if I can spot the fake," Sara summed up. "Better assign a detective for the legwork."

Trying to look like a Civil War hobbyist, Sara sat on a hard chair and made notes as the auctioneer knocked down one ancient-looking item after another. There were tattered Confederate battle flags, a curved sword in a flaking leather scabbard, a moth-eaten khaki overcoat with captain's bars on the shoulders, a pair of engraved cavalry spurs, a torn copy of a love letter datelined Gettysburg, and dozens of other nostalgic reminders of the past. Sara stayed for it all, even bidding on a silver buckle from some long-dead officer's belt. But long before she left, she had signaled the young detective to follow one of the successful bidders as soon as he claimed his purchase. And that night the Star of Sharaze was on its way back to its actress-owner.

Which of the Civil War items was a fake?

The khaki coat, of course. The Civil War was fought between "the blue and the gray." — Union officers in blue uniforms, Southern in gray. Khaki was adopted by the U.S. Army later.

23 / THE FORGOTTEN
FIVE HUNDRED

People leave everything in library books — everything flat, that is. Sara Hull and her assistant librarians had found lottery tickets, theater tickets, love letters, poison-pen letters, bills, even a marriage license. And, sometimes, they found money. But not usually as much money as Chuck Westerly found one afternoon when he came to work after school. He found five hundred dollars.

For a few minutes he debated whether to turn it in or not. After all, he was human. But there was something about the money. It had funny vibes. And it looked funny too. The way it was folded. Three hundred dollar bills were folded in a sort of fan shape. Two fifties had all four corners turned down. And the five twenties were folded in half, with two corners turned down.

"I'm not George Washington or Abe Lincoln or

anybody — but I found this," and he held the bills out to Sara Hull. "If — well, if nobody claims it — ?"

"I think it will be yours," Sara said. "But first hand me that telephone book, will you please?"

The money had been between the pages of a popular novel being read that month by everyone in the country, from college professors to sanitation men. The population of the city numbered several thousand people. But Sara Hull dialed a number, asked for the director. "Have any of your people reported anything lost recently?" she asked after identifying herself. Chuck could hear the excitement in the voice at the other end of the line. "Mr. Bascomb," Sara repeated. "Well, it'll be here any time he can come and identify it."

A few hours later a man walking with the aid of a cane came up to the library desk. "I'm Arthur Bascomb," he said. "I've been taking that book back and forth to the Center for reading, and stuck the money in it for safekeeping. A friend returned it for me the other day, and when I missed the money, I just never thought of it. I've been sick about it — banks are a lot of trouble, but I've learned my lesson." He described the precise way in which the bills were folded.

When the money was placed in his hand, Mr. Bascomb asked, "Who found it?" Sara pushed Chuck forward, and Bascomb slipped one of the fifty dollar bills into his hand. "Oh, no, sir, I couldn't, honest," Chuck protested. "You gave me a fifty-dollar bill — did you mean to?"

"I only wish it could be more," Mr. Bascomb

said. "After all, you didn't do it because you knew me — you did it because you were honest, and that's a lot better reason."

How did Sara know where to call about the money?

She called the Volunteer Readers for the Blind. Blind people often tell bills apart by folding each denomination in a special way.

24 / THE AUSTRALIAN FIANCÉ

"I know it's silly at my time of life," twittered Agatha Conybeare, her silver-blue curls bobbing as she told Sara about her new fiancé. "But Sara, he's just wonderful! That marvelous Cockney accent! An Australian sheep farmer with literally miles of land — my money doesn't mean a thing to him. I can't wait until you meet him!"

Sitting across the tea table from Hilary Fensham, Sara admitted that Agatha had made a delightful choice. He was big, hearty, masculine, yet attentive and sensitive. His broad accent added to his charm, and his English tweed coat and gold cuff links seemed to prove Agatha's assurance that money had nothing to do with his offer of marriage.

As they got to know each other better, Hilary began to talk about his business. "Fine sheep," he said with pride. "We produce the wool that goes into the finest angora scarves and sweaters made in the world." He went on to describe the wonders of Australia — the Great Barrier Reef, the outback, the freedom and prosperity of the people.

When Agatha went for more water, Sara looked at Hilary sadly.

"Hilary, I like you," she said. "And Agatha's one of my oldest friends and I want her to be happy after all these years of loneliness. I think you may really love her."

"I do." Hilary's sincerity seemed beyond doubt. "I like — well, birdlike little women. My first wife was one."

"But I guess she didn't leave you much money, did she?" Sara said. "Hilary, tell Agatha the truth. Tell her where you really come from — maybe it *is* Australia. But you don't raise sheep. Give her a chance to make up her mind knowing who you really are and what you really do."

Why did Sara doubt Hilary?

Angora doesn't come from sheep — it comes from goats and rabbits. Agatha wore a scarf made out of it when she married Hilary, who thought it was more romantic to play the role of a sheep rancher rather than tractor salesman.

25 / THE BOLD BIOGRAPHER

"Sara Hull, I've done it!" The tall young man waved a tape recorder case in Sara's face, his face beaming. "Please — let me play you some of the interview. If I don't let somebody hear it, I'll explode!"

Sara laughed, and gestured toward her office. Ten years before, Arnold Morris had been the brightest, brashest reporter on the high school paper, always full of angles for stories which he poured out to her as he sorted books in the library after school. But his career hadn't panned out as brilliantly as he'd expected. He had had a mediocre book published and had sold a few stories to magazines, but his name was hardly a household word. For the past two weeks he'd been in town poring over the library's files on Lemuel Lamb, the billionaire recluse who had lived in total seclusion in a mansion ten miles away for fifteen of his sixty years. Sara had recognized the symptoms. Arnold wasn't the first writer who had tried to interview the elusive Lamb. But now he seemed to be the first one who had succeeded.

She was excited herself as Arnold plugged in the machine and a flat, Western-accented voice began to speak. "I won't play it all, of course," Arnold grinned, "just a few choice parts of it." As he flipped the switches and pressed buttons, the voice answered questions about a twenty-million dollar deal that had, until now, been a mystery to every financier in the world.

"Isn't this terrific?" Arnold was nearly jumping up and down with enthusiasm. "But that's nothing. You know how he's always been a woman hater — never dated anybody, never married — as far as anyone knew. Well, he *was* married! When he was twenty-two — back during the Depression when he was just finding out how to make money. Listen!"

Lamb's voice sounded sad. "Never cared for any woman after she got killed," he was telling Arnold on the tape. "We ran away and got married. She was a poor kid — America was still a sick country, economically, in 1934, in spite of Roosevelt and all that. I wanted to give her everything — it wasn't considered proper, but I bought her a pair of nylon stockings to wear to our wedding — they were hard to get back then — and a little hat with a blue feather, and a white sillk blouse to wear with her blue suit. And, of course, a corsage — white gardenias. It was winter — cold

— I made up my mind she'd have a mink coat, too, before that winter was over. That's why I started to make money — to buy her the things I wanted her to have —"

Sara Hull reached over and turned off the tape recorder.

"Sorry, Arnold," she said, "it won't work. Lemuel Lamb never said any of that — and you'll get in real trouble if you try to sell it as an interview with him. Who acted the part of Lamb — one of your friends?"

What made Sara doubt the tape?

Nylon hadn't been marketed yet in 1934. Nylon stockings weren't just hard to get, they were nonexistent.

26 / THE HUSBAND'S DIARY

"Sara, do you know a good lawyer? I'm thinking of suing Donald for divorce."

"But Karen, I thought you were so happy —" Sara Hull gasped in astonishment.

"I did too. Oh, we've had spats because he travels so much and I have to stay home, but I always thought he was faithful to me. But you know that business trip he took to Dublin last month? Well, he kept a travel diary. Never showed it to me, said it was all about business. Yesterday I was getting some clothes ready to send to the cleaner, and found it in one of his pockets. Just for fun, I looked through it — and Sara, he spent all his time with another woman! It wasn't just business — he even met her mother! Probably they thought they'd caught a rich, unmarried American — or just didn't care. Look at it!" She held out a

72

small, red-bound book. "Her name is Florence Shanrahan. 'Florence met me at the airport.' 'We went to the Shanrahan ancestral home — Mrs. Shanrahan is a real aristocrat.'" Karen sniffled. "He thinks *my* mother is just a silly old woman. 'Florence and I had dinner in a real Irish pub.' 'Florence took me to the horse show.' And this — this is the final insult: 'Florence and Mrs. Shanrahan helped me pick out a nice Waterford vase — it'll help make it up to Karen.' I'll bet he didn't tell Florence's mother who Karen was! Oh, Sara!"

Sara Hull touched her friend's hand. "Have you asked Donald about this woman?" she said. Karen shook her head. "Well, before you do anything stupid, show him this book and ask him who Florence Shanrahan is. But first, let me tell you something you obviously don't know, so you'll be more likely to believe what he tells you."

That night Sara answered her telephone to hear Karen's ecstatic voice. "Oh, thank you for telling me that! Donald even showed me snapshots of the Shanrahans — he'd just had them developed. I could have made such a mess of everything — it was all business, of course. Sara, I can never begin to thank you enough."

What did Sara tell Karen?

In Ireland, Florence is a name often given to men. Mrs. Shanrahan was Florence's wife.

73

27 / WHO KILLED MRS. HIGGINS?

"Can you tell us who did it, Mrs. Higgins?" Detective Inspector Bill Tawson bent over the hospital bed as the old woman's mouth moved.

"It was — the — Andy," Mrs. Higgins whispered, a look of fear flickering in her dim eyes. "My cameo — the — it was — Andy —" Her voice trailed off. A white-capped nurse stepped forward. "She must rest if she's to have any chance at all," she said. Bill nodded and left the hospital. An hour later he was told that Mrs. Higgins had died, victim of an attacker who had surprised her in her room, ripped off her cameo brooch, rummaged through her bureau drawers, and escaped. The police were questioning Andy Higgins, her grandson.

"I tell you I loved my grandmother!" the young

man protested. "She was one of those independent old Englishwomen, a Cockney — had gone to work at the age of 13, and wouldn't stop. She'd come to America to work for the Van Alstons fifty years ago, and she was still cooking and cleaning, though we begged her to quit. We told her they were away too much, for one thing — like last night, when she was all alone on that big estate. There aren't any other servants now, except the handyman, Leach, and some girls who help with special parties, and a woman who does the heavy housework. My grandmother was always saying how different they were from the people she used to work with in the old days. Yes, I did go to see her for awhile that night, but I was home hours before it happened — my wife will tell you that. My grandmother couldn't have said I did it!"

"I can't believe she said it, either," said Sara Hull, putting down the newspaper in which she had just read the Higgins story.

"We've checked everyone she knew." Bill answered. "Her grandson was the only person she had anything to do with who had a name anything like Andy. And everything she owned was going to him in her will. She owned quite a bit too — some very good jewelry, besides that cameo, and she'd been a shrewd investor in the stock market all these years. Andy's wife isn't well, and there's the baby — He hasn't worked steadily for a year and he was there that night and she named him."

"Aren't there any other suspects? Wasn't anyone else around?"

"George Leach, the Van Alstons' jack-of-all-trades, was on the premises and might have thought the old lady had some money in her room," Bill said. "But she'd hardly have called George Leach by her grandson's name — and she was rational, Sara, the doctors agreed."

"Of course she was rational," Sara said. "And George Leach was the very person she was naming. Search his room, and I'll bet you'll find some of her property."

Sara was right — but why?

Old Mrs. Higgins was a lower-class English-woman, who dropped her *h's*. She was trying to say "the — handyman —." But it came out "the — 'andy —."

28 / MURDER IN
THE CANDY STORE

Outside Marty and Louie's candy shop a curious crowd had gathered to watch an ambulance team carry out a stretcher. On it a motionless figure lay, shrouded from head to toe in a brown blanket.

"I'd better look into this," Bill Tawson said to Sara Hull, pulling his car up to the curb. "I know you'll come with me, whatever I say." The detective inspector and the librarian stepped out of the automobile and crossed the street to the shop. A flash of Bill's badge, and the young policeman standing guard let them enter the narrow room, where a short squat man with a few strands of hair combed over his nearly bald skull was standing in front of a case filled with cheap candy.

"I was in the washroom in back when it happened," he was telling the two plainclothes detectives who stood beside him, notebooks open. "I was just combin' my hair when I heard the doorbell jangle, and then Marty let out a yell. I rushed out and seen a young punk at the cash register. When he seen me he lit out and ran off. I couldn't follow him, 'cause I seen the blood coming out of Marty's throat. He was down on the floor — I tried to stop it — " he held up hands reddened with blood " — but I couldn't do nothin', so I called you guys."

"Oh, dear." The detectives looked sourly at Sara, and even Bill frowned as she held up a hand smeared with white, gooey candy. "I wasn't watching what I was doing and squeezed one of those pieces of candy in the dish on top of the counter," she explained with embarrassment. "May I go back to the washroom and clean up?" The detectives bristled and Louie looked outraged, but Bill nodded and Sara pushed her way past the men and went through the doorway at the rear of the shop. A few seconds later she returned, holding something out to Bill.

"Here it is, Bill," she said. "I knew you'd want it. As you can see, it's empty — not a strand in it." Turning to the candy seller she asked, "What did you do with the knife after you killed your partner?"

What did Sara find in the washroom?

78

She found a comb — clean, not a strand of hair in it. If the candy seller, whose hair was falling out, had been combing it when he heard his partner call, there would have been hair in the comb.

29 / THE TRAVELING RIVAL

"What's the matter, Steve?" Sara looked fondly at her favorite after-school library assistant. "Is it Jenny? Competition from that new senior, Vic Rambeau?"

"Yeah, you're right — as usual," Steve admitted. "Vic says he's been everywhere and seen all the places Jenny's always wanted to go to. I've never been farther away than Washington, D.C. That gives him what I guess you call charisma."

"Sounds like Othello and Desdemona," Sara commented. "She loved him for the dangers he'd passed; Jenny loves Vic for the cities he's passed through."

Later, looking for a book on one of the shelves, Sara heard two familiar voices in the next stack. One of the voices' conversation was confined to, "Gee!" "Oh, Vic, it must be wonderful there!"

Vic Rambeau was, as usual, holding forth about his travels.

"When you have a smattering of one or two languages, you find words that are just like words in other languages — almost, anyway. For instance, Russia. Russian isn't anything like French, or Italian, or English — but words like sugar and baggage, and restaurant sound a lot alike. You get so you can figure out street signs, and headlines, and stuff. I remember one night I was lost in Moscow, and was getting hungry. Up ahead I saw a sign that said "Restaurant," and was I glad! I just . . ."

Back at the main desk, Sara waited until Vic and a starry-eyed Jenny emerged. Steve kept his eyes determinedly on his work, but he might have been in Moscow himself for all Jenny seemed to notice. "Vic," Sara called, "could you come over here for a second?" She held out a piece of paper on which she had printed the word *pectopah*. "I understand you've been to Russia — do you know what this word means? And how to pronounce it?"

Vic studied the paper. "Gosh, Miss Hull," he said, "I don't know what it means. I don't really know Russian. I think I'd accent the middle syllable, though — " with an exaggerated Russian accent he said "peck-TOE-paw" as Jenny giggled admiringly. Sara shook her head.

"Are you sure you've really been to Russia, Vic?" she said bluntly. Steve's head lifted. Vic blushed scarlet and Jenny looked shocked as Sara explained why she was pretty sure Vic had never been lost — or found — in Moscow.

How did Sara know?

Vic was right — some Russian words do sound like English words. But Russians use the Cyrillic alphabet, which is quite different from ours, so words don't *look* alike. P means r, c can be pronounced like our s, h means n. So the word *pecto- pah* — as Vic would have known if he'd seen it on a sign and gone there to eat — means, and is pronounced "restaurant."

30 / THE LIBRARY CARD KILLER

"It's one of those sick patterns," Bill Tawson said, looking sick himself. "Every girl the guy has killed has been found with a library book beside her, taken out on a temporary card from the local library. Fingerprints match on the books and the card applications, but descriptions from the librarians don't. They all agree that the killer is about five feet eight and weighs about 150 — like half the men on the street. They all think he's between 30 and 35 years old. But one says he had a red mustache, one that he had long blond hair like a hippie, one that he looked like a perfect young executive. Sometimes he wore glasses, sometimes not. He filled out some of the applications in his own handwriting, some in block printing, took one somewhere and had it typed and returned it. But he's killed five girls in college towns, each a month apart, working down from the border — which makes us next.

"So, Sara, we're taking over your office while you man — or I should say 'woman' — the main desk. What we want you to do is stall on all card applications. Ask everybody to take a seat and wait while your secretary types up the temporary cards — girls and old ladies, too, in case the guy is watching. That old man studying religious texts over there is really a police officer, and so is the fat housewife reading the fashion magazines. And the 'secretary' who comes out and picks up the applications will be taking them to check the handwriting and the fingerprints. But you've had more experience with those forms than we have — so if you'd give every one a quick once-over and pin a note on any that seem even faintly suspicious — any phony information — you might save us some important time."

It seemed to Sara Hull that every man who applied for a library card that week was between 30 and 35, five feet eight inches tall, and was possibly wearing a wig. Then, on Thursday, at about three o'clock, she saw it. In front of her the card application form of Roger D'Arciman, formerly of Magnolia, Minnesota, now living at the Summit Hotel, graduate of John F. Kennedy High School in 1959, two years at Iowa State, salesman for an electronics company. He gave as references a doctor in Iowa and three teachers in Minnesota. Hastily, Sara scribbled a note, pinned it to the form, and punched the buzzer that summoned her policewoman secretary.

"He'd already made a date for tonight with a switchboard operator at the hotel," Bill Tawson told Sara later. "Was just waiting to pick out the ritual library book — then kill number six. Thanks a lot for your help, Sherlock girl."

What was wrong with D'Arciman's application?

President John F. Kennedy wasn't elected until 1960, was assassinated in 1963. Before that time, high schools weren't named for him.

31 / THE FURTIVE FUGITIVES

It wasn't cold in the seaside hotel room, but Sara Hull shivered from excitement. She believed that she had recognized the good-looking young couple who had come up in the elevator with her, and gone into the room next to hers. The girl's hair was arranged differently from the way Sara remembered it on a recent TV news broadcast, and both the man and woman had worn enormous sunglasses. But there was something about the girl's mouth and her walk that reminded Sara of the film that had been shown, made when Veronica Cotter was a teacher at a big university. Now she was wanted in connection with a bombing in which three people had been killed. Was she in the room next door with her also much-photographed and much-wanted husband?

"I don't want to call the police and have them disturb some perfectly innocent young couple who may really need a vacation at the shore," Sara thought. "If only I could make out what they're saying — it might give me a clue." But all she could hear through the hotel wall was a slur of voices, the words indistinguishable. Feeling like a supersnoop, Sara tried pressing a water glass against the pink wallpaper, but could decipher nothing definite.

Suddenly she had an inspiration. In a weak, strained little voice, she made a request over the phone to the hotel's desk clerk. Half an hour later, answering a knock at the door, Sara admitted a well-dressed, middle-aged man carrying a small black bag. She explained her suspicions to him. For a moment he hesitated, then shrugged. "They do it on TV," she said, "it might work. After all, it can't really hurt anybody, can it? Except Veronica Cotter and her husband, and if they're next door, it's our duty to turn them in."

Neither he nor Sara Hull left the room. But within fifteen minutes they were sure that the man and woman in the next room were indeed the Cotters. "Ronnie" and "Dave," they called each other, as they discussed plans for catching a plane for Argentina where they would be safe from prosecution. Sara's companion placed the call to the police. And that night the capture of the notorious Cotters was the headline story on every TV news show.

Who was the man Sara called? How did they identify the Cotters?

Sara called a doctor, who placed his stethoscope against the wall and they heard everything that went on in the next room.

32 / HIT-RUN AND
UNCLE HORATIO

The white-haired old priest smiled as he shook hands with Sara Hull in the hospital waiting room.

"Your uncle Horatio will make a complete recovery, don't worry for a moment," he told her. "He's still dazed and shocked — how could a driver strike another human being with an automobile and not even stop? The doctors don't want him to have visitors yet — I happened to be here when he was brought into the emergency room, and they let me see him. Wonderful spirit — wonderful faith. He keeps saying, 'God willing, I'll live to be 100.' Over and over — 'God willing, 100.'"

Sara looked surprised. Uncle Horatio was the least religious of all the Hulls, and the most pessimistic. She would have expected him to resign himself to death if he stubbed his toe, not make inspirational statements.

"Are you sure Uncle Horatio said that, Father Lanahan?" she asked.

"Oh, yes. He said it in Latin — the abbreviation,

that is. I know what he means. When you get to our age, living to be 100 is our ambition, whatever you may hear us say. Well, I must go now. I'll drop by again — perhaps we'll meet."

A few minutes later, driving away from the hospital, Sara found the priest's words running through her mind. It wasn't Uncle Horatio Hull's style. Far more like him to curse the unknown hit-and-run driver whom the police, so far, had not found. Just then a green car pulled suddenly out of a side street, making an illegal turn and almost grazing Sara's automobile. Automatically, Sara's eyes dropped to the fender — and she gasped. Pulling up to the curb, she almost ran the few feet to a telephone booth and dialed the police, asking for her friend, Detective Inspector Bill Tawson.

"Bill, Bill," she cried excitedly. "I've just spotted the car that hit Uncle Horatio — it's going west on Broad Street, a green — " Her description was detailed enough to result in the capture of the motorist, and marks on the car proved, unmistakably, that Uncle Horatio Hull had been his victim.

"Don't give me the credit," Sara said to Bill. "Uncle Horatio is the one — he told Father Lanahan who to look for!"

How did Horatio help?

By giving the car's license number — DV 100. D.V. means *Deo volente*, or God willing, in Latin, and is often used — but not by skeptics like Horatio Hull.

33 / THE FOLLOWED FRIEND

"Shut the door, please, Sara. I'm afraid someone will hear."

Obligingly, Sara Hull shut the door of her office in the public library. Shirley Yerby moved her chair to the least conspicuous corner, her mouth working nervously.

"Someone is following me," she explained in a hoarse, frightened whisper. "Oh, Sara, call Bill Tawson, please."

"I will, but tell me what to tell him," Sara pulled her telephone closer, but did not lift the receiver.

"Well, you know I have to go to business luncheons — it's part of my job at the store. The kind where they feed you, but at the same time give a pitch for the product they want you to stock — you know the kind. Well, today there was a big one, full scale, at the Hotel Dollinger. I won't go into the details — "

"Yes, you will," said Sara. "Tell me exactly what happened, from the time you went in."

"Oh, all right. I went to the hotel, took the elevator to the Gladiola Room where the luncheon was being held. They had tables set up outside the room — you know, secretaries check to make sure you're invited, give you a plastic name tag to pin on, and a big portfolio full of advertising for the product. This was a new kind of laundry hamper, put out by Silkwick — I went into the Gladiola Room with the folder under my arm, had a drink at the bar, then sat down at the table for lunch. I sat between two old friends — Mary Loll from Americo Advertising and Tim Sage from *House-to-House* magazine. We had some kind of Italian dish — lasagna, I think — then the Silkwick people got up and told us how wonderful the hamper was, and after that we all said 'see ya' and left. I felt sort of sleepy from the big lunch, and decided to go home instead of back to work — it was nearly four. Well, I got on the bus, and that's when it happened. This big red-haired man got on. He came over to me, looked me right in the face, and said, 'Hello, Miss Yerby.' Then he went and sat in the back. I was scared to death. Sara, I swear, he wasn't at that luncheon. I didn't meet him there; never saw him before in my life. Well, I didn't get off at my stop — I went one beyond. And sure enough, he got off when I did. He went the other way — I suppose he doubled back, but — well, that's not all. I walked around the block, then made a rush for my house. I got inside the hall and a man — another one I'd never seen — was coming out. He smiled and he spoke to me too: 'Miss Yerby, how are you?' Sara, please call Bill. They're after me for something. I don't know what, but how did those men know my name if they haven't been put on my trail? Please, Sara."

Sara stood up, and held out her hand to her friend.

"I'll call Bill, but first I want you to come over here," she said. She guided Shirley to the far corner of the room, and pointed to the wall. "Look," she said. "Take a good look. See it? Do you still want me to call the Detective Bureau?"

What did Sara point to?

A mirror. Shirley had forgotten to take off the name tag that had been given to her before the luncheon — the men had simply read her name and called her by it for fun.

34 / TRUTH AND
THE SON-IN-LAW

Sara glowed as she sat in the living room of her friend, Glenda Morro, and listened to Glenda's new son-in-law talk about his father. Glenda glowed, too, and Anita, the bride, seemed to shine as she looked at Max.

"My father was an artist," the handsome young man was saying, "a sort of wanderer, I suppose, but he gave me an understanding of life that was like an understanding of painting — color, creativity, freedom, freshness of viewpoint. I hope to be able to give that to my children too." And he looked adoringly at his wife.

A few days later Sara sat in a booth in the Country Restaurant and heard the same deep young voice talking to someone in the booth behind her. More important, she was having lunch with Glenda Morro, who started to rise when she heard her son-in-law, then stiffened as she caught the drift of his conversation.

"I grew up on a college campus," Max was telling his unseen companion. "Shaded by the groves of academe. Very strong standards, a bit narrow, not much freedom, but good in its way. I'm the son of a professor of classics — learned Greek instead of nursery rhymes. Not much money but impeccable social position. I hope I can give my children the same sense of who they are, where they belong, the same dedication to the intellectual life I was brought up with — "

Glenda's face was pale.

"Sara, he's lying," she whispered. "Anita married him in such a short time I didn't know much about him until the day you were there. And now he's telling a different story."

"Let's slip out without his seeing us and go to the library," Sara said. "I've some directories in my office that may settle this. His name is Max Whitlock, Jr., so we should be able to find out if the father is a professor, at least. I don't blame you — " suddenly she stopped. "Come on," she said in a different tone. "I've just thought of something. Anita's happiness may depend on it."

An hour later, Sara and Glenda looked at each other across an open directory.

"At least there's one thing Anita won't have to face," Sara said.

What was it?

Male chauvinism. Max's *mother* was the classics professor.

94

35 / A MUGGING ON MARBLE STREET

"There was another bad mugging last night," Rick Fredrix reported, his face serious. "Rose Banning's mother — you know Rose, Miss Hull. Mrs. Banning's still in the hospital, unconscious. Rose says she thinks they'll have to operate."

"What happened this time?" Sara asked.

"Well, Rose had Bernie Mell over to study with, and Mrs. Banning said she needed some exercise and would walk the dog — that's usually Rose's job. Nobody knows what happened, of course— she was crazy to go down Marble Street, where it's dark and that empty lot and all, but she did, 'cause that's where they found her. Imagine, she was just walking along, whistling a little tune, with the dog off the leash, and all of a sudden — the guy must have jumped her. The dog started barking loud, and howling, and ran up to Central

Road and somebody saw him and called the cops and — there she was. Gosh, I'm glad it wasn't my mom."

"People are so foolish to take chances like that," Sara said. "But now, we've got to do some work. Take this reference room slip back to Miss Stevenson, will you, please?" Rick bounded up the stairs, and Sara lifted the telephone, dialed, and asked for Detective Inspector Tawson.

"Bill," she said, "someone from the police had better come over here. I hate to tell you, but I think I know who mugged Mrs. Banning last night."

Was it Rick?

Of course. How could he have known that Mrs. Banning was whistling as she walked the dog, if no one had been anywhere around and she was still unconscious?

36 / THE LADY
FROM HONOLULU

"Sally, girl, I'd like you to meet Mrs. Carrel."
Horatio Hull rose as Sara paused to acknowledge
the introduction before sitting down in the third
seat at the restaurant table. "You don't remember
her, do you?"

"No, I'm afraid not." Sara studied the woman's
carefully made-up face, her chic clothes. "Have
we met before?"

"I was in high school when you were," Mrs.
Carrel laughed. "Oh, I was a freshman when you
were a senior — but I lived here for six months
with my aunt, Affinia Sinceau." Her face grew
grave. "Poor Aunt Affinia. All those years alone.
I hope she's at peace at last. I went back home to
Honolulu after the Christmas holidays that year,
and have never been back — I feel a little guilty,
since she's been so generous to me, but — " she

shrugged. "Marriage, problems of various kinds —
my maiden name was Bess Hamilton, by the way."

"Yes, of course, I remember," Sara said. "Not
well — but a girl from Hawaii was quite a novelty
in those days. Like someone from the tropics —
it must have seemed very cold to you here in
the north that winter."

"Oh, I shivered," Mrs. Carrel admitted. "But
I'd never seen snow, and it was so beautiful. To
think I've inherited that lovely old house, and
the grounds. I remember the maple tree outside
my window that winter, how the green leaves
sparkled against the white snow. And the pines
stood so straight and dark and tall, and how we
burned the branches in the fireplace and the whole
house smelled fragrant for hours. Aunt Affinia had
an old sleigh, and we went riding in it — I wonder
if it's still there in the barn? Your Uncle Horatio
was Aunt Affinia's lawyer, you know, and I just got
word about the will and flew right over. I haven't
been out to the estate yet, we've been discussing
the money — I mean the other part of the legacy.
Oh, dear, I've spilled my coffee on my glove. Will
you excuse me for a moment while I go and try
to wash it out?"

As Mrs. Carrel hurried toward the powder room,
Sara looked hard at Uncle Horatio Hull.

"Uncle Horatio," she said firmly, "that isn't the
real Bess Hamilton. She has obviously found out,
either from Bess or from some other source, a lot
about Affinia Sinceau and her home. But she
never spent the winter here when she was in school
— she looks a little like the Bess I remember,

98

but she's not Bess. You'd better start doing some investigating to find the real heir."

What was wrong with "Bess's" story?

Maple trees change color in fall, then shed their leaves. In winter a maple tree would have had dark branches outlined against the snow, not green leaves.

37 / THE SULLEN MOVER

"I just need these boxes taken out to my car," Sara Hull explained to the shaggy-haired teenaged boy. She wasn't much impressed by Rocky Easton's attitude, and she knew he was tough — he had a police record for minor offenses. But he was the only boy who had responded to the advertisement for help she had posted on the library bulletin board, and she decided to trust him. Movers were due the next day, but she wanted to drive some of her possessions to her new apartment this morning to save the professionals' time.

Nevertheless, as Rocky shifted his gum and slouched unenthusiastically toward the pile of boxes, Sara was relieved to hear the jangle of her doorbell. She was a little disconcerted to find her friend, Bill Tawson of the detective bureau, at the door, especially when Rocky stiffened and shot her a look of outrage.

"Sorry to interrupt," Bill said, showing his badge, "but I'm afraid this is official." Sensing Rocky's suspicion, he added, "Miss Hull has nothing to do with this visit, Rocky. Your mother told me where to find you."

"Whatta the fuzz want with me now?" Rocky snarled. "I'm clean — I ain't done nothin."

"Just a few questions," Bill proceeded. "You used to work for the Discount All-Nite Drug Store as a delivery boy, didn't you?"

"Yeah," Rocky admitted. "But the probation officer made me quit because I hadda work after midnight. Whatta ya on my back for — I never stole a dime!"

"I didn't say you did," Bill said patiently. "But you made two deliveries while you worked there to Mrs. Hartman's house, didn't you?"

"Who's Mrs. Hartman? I don't remember everybody I took stuff to," Rocky answered evasively.

"Oh, come on, Rocky, you didn't have that much to do." Bill looked annoyed. "A big house over on Chestnut Street. White, sits back from the street."

"Oh, that place." Rocky seemed to reconsider. "Old dame — I remember. Not bad, useta give a decent tip for a change. Yeah, I took orders there a couple of nights. Never went in, though. Just waited in the hall for the money." He became suddenly communicative, as if deciding on cooperation. "Weird kinda place. I could see into the living room. Purple walls, real dark, and white

101

furniture." Suspicion reappeared. "What's this all about?"

"Okay, I'll level with you. Early this morning old Mrs. Hartman was beaten up when she found someone robbing the house. A neighbor heard her screaming, and saw a boy who answers your description running away from the house. How about it?"

Rocky swelled up like a furious toad. "Listen, copper," he yelled. "You can't pin nothing on me! Just because I got a record you pigs try to pin everything on me! I never been to that old dame's house except to make two deliveries at night — I never been there any day, today, or any day!"

Sara looked at him sadly.

"Rocky," she said, "that's not true. You must have been at Miss Hartman's house during the day. I'd like to believe you, but you're just not telling the truth."

How did Sara know?

Purple walls look brown at night. To know they were really purple, Rocky would have had to see Mrs. Hartman's living room walls in daylight.

38 / CRIME IN THE SUN

Afternoon sun streamed through the high, shadeless library windows. In the reading section, it turned the hair of the packed-in teenagers studying for exams to gold, platinum, and copper. It made a prism of librarian Sara Hull's glass pencil holder, and illuminated the almost invisible line across the middle of the eyeglass lenses of the tall, fair teenager waiting in line to fill out a request slip at the desk. With the sun in their eyes, the students were having trouble filling out the slips, and Sara watched with exasperation as the boy fumbled when his turn came — her exasperation was not with the boy but with the library's tight budget.

"Money or no money," she thought as the boy knocked over a pile of books on the crowded tables, "we've got to have more space, and window shades too." She looked up from filing the slips to be half-blinded by a sudden, tiny flash of light — the sun on a police badge. A young plainclothesman stood at the desk, holding open his coat so that only she could see the shield.

"Bad mugging over on Elm Street, Miss Hull," he said matter-of-factly, as if asking about a book. "Old man in his eighties, knocked unconscious, probably robbed. Put up a terrific fight — glasses smashed on the ground beside him, skinned knuckles, but the punk got away. Storekeeper said he was a tall, blond guy, looked like he might have been a teenager, running toward the library. Any kids in here today?"

"Look," Sara indicated the rows of studying young people. "It's exam time — there must be at least thirty-five or more. But from what you say, I think I can point out the right one." Almost imperceptibly, she slanted a pencil toward the tall boy in glasses, sitting at the end of a table with a book open in front of him. "Try not to make too much noise when you arrest him, will you?"

How could Sara Hull be so sure?

The boy was wearing bifocal glasses — almost never prescribed for anyone under 40. Sara reasoned that he must have picked up the old man's glasses by mistake when his own were smashed in the struggle — especially logical thinking since he seemed to have trouble with his vision.

39 / THE DEATH OF
THE NEW TENANT

"I won't be in this afternoon, Miss Hull." At the other end of the telephone line Diane Lesser's voice sounded shaken. "Something terrible happened at our house — I didn't even go to school, I'm so upset. You know we rent out the apartment on the third floor. Well, we rented it last week to a woman who seemed sort of sad, but nice. She was supposed to move in today, and she came last night with a sleeping bag and asked if she could spend the night there to wait for her furniture — it was coming from another town, she said. My mother said okay and gave her the key — there wasn't any furniture at all up there, not a single thing, but she said she'd manage just for one night. Mother offered her a chair, but she said she didn't need it.

"Well, this morning Mother went up to see if she'd like to come down and have some breakfast with us — and — and — " Diane's voice choked, and she was barely able to continue. "Oh, it was awful. I was right in back of Mother when she knocked on the door — it swung open — the woman hadn't even locked it — and — she was hanging, Miss Hull. Hanging from the light fixture in the middle of the room! She used a belt — her face was all purple — her feet were just swinging there in the empty space — oh, I'm sorry, Miss Hull, I can't help crying —"

"Diane, what did the police say?" Sara's voice was sharp.

"They said people do that sometimes — rent a hotel room or an apartment just to — to — commit suicide in. They know somebody'll find them that way — if they live alone and do it in their own homes nobody finds them for a long time sometimes. We gave them her name, but it was like they thought — she didn't have any family, she told us —"

"Diane, I'm going to hang up now," Sara said. "But someone from the detective bureau will probably be over there. I'm calling the Inspector now — tell your mother. If what you've told me is right, your tenant didn't commit suicide — she was murdered."

Why did Sara doubt the suicide?

If there was no furniture in the room, the woman would have had nothing to stand on in order to reach the light fixture from which she supposedly hung herself. Someone else must have lifted her there — the person who went out, leaving the door unlocked.

106

40 / THE WOMEN'S LIBBER

"Who would ever have imagined when Hetty Weeden and I were roommates at college," Sara Hull thought as she pushed the doorbell of Hetty's hotel suite, "that I'd wind up a town librarian and she'd be the world's most famous Women's Liberationist? Oh, well — " The door opened, but instead of her friend, Sara faced a tall young brunette in a brown tailored suit.

"Yes?" the girl said coldly.

"I'm Sara Hull," the librarian explained. "Hetty is expecting me."

"Really?" said the girl, with an air of surprise. "How strange. Miss Weeden left about fifteen minutes ago. She said she'd be gone most of the day. I'm her secretary, Miss Angela Smithers. Are you sure you have an appointment?"

"Why, yes, I talked to her only half an hour

ago," Sara answered. "She said to come over as soon as I could."

"Well, I'm afraid I can't help you. May I have your name again?"

"Sara Hull."

"Miss Hull or Mrs. Hull?" Sara frowned at the girl's question, but replied, "Miss."

"Well, all I can say, Miss Hull," Angela smiled politely, "is that I'll tell Miss Weeden you were here and ask her to get in touch with you if she does come back. Does she know where to reach you?"

"Yes, she does. Thank you," Sara said, as Angela Smithers nodded and shut the door. Sara stood still for a moment, thinking. Then, instead of going to the elevator, she stepped around a corner where she could watch the door but not be seen from it. She had only a few minutes to wait until Angela Smithers stepped into the hall, an attaché case in her hand. Carefully locking the door, she looked swiftly up and down the corridor, then walked quickly to a large potted plant and thrust the room key into the soil around it. With another quick glance around her, she moved to the elevator and pushed the button, tapping her foot impatiently until the car arrived and she disappeared inside.

Hastily, Sara jumped from her hiding place, hurried to the plant, retrieved the key, unlocked the suite door. "Hetty?" she called, running through the tiny foyer into the living room. The room was empty, and the door to the adjoining bedroom was closed. Sara rushed to it and pushed it open. There, on the bedroom floor, lay her friend, face down, the back of her blonde hair disfigured with a spreading bloodstain. Hetty moaned as Sara knelt at her side, reaching across her body to lift the receiver from the phone on the night table.

"There's been an accident," she said. "Send a doctor to Hetty Weeden's room at once. And then connect me with Detective Inspector Bill Tawson's office at police headquarters — that's right — Tawson. And hurry!"

Miraculously, it seemed only seconds until Bill's voice crackled at the other end of the wire. "Bill," Sara said, her firm voice beginning to break at last, "Hetty Weeden's been attacked by a woman posing as her secretary. She was tall, with long dark hair, wearing a brown tweed suit. Yes, yes, I'm sure she was an imposter — she couldn't really have worked for Hetty, that's why I wanted you to check up on her. She didn't know anything, anything at all, about the Women's Liberation movement!"

How did Sara know Angela was lying?

No self-respecting women's libber would have stressed "Mrs." and "Miss" as Angela did. Women's liberationists are in favor of dropping both forms of address, possibly substituting "Ms.," or using first names entirely.

41 / THANKSGIVING DINNER

Loneliness and need were the only prices of admission. As she did every Thanksgiving Day before joining her family, Sara Hull was helping serve dinner at the city mission. Gleaming white tablecloths, flowers, shining silver, gave the hall the air of a smart restaurant. But the patrons exuded a common aura of defeat. Most were men, though there was a scattering of tired-looking women. Most were gray-haired, quiet, with faces that looked frightened whenever they stopped smiling. But today, at least, there was something to smile about.

Sara was about to take a tray of turkey and all the fixings from the kitchen when she heard Bill Tawson's voice at her elbow.

"Sara," the detective inspector said in a low tone, "we've got the place staked out. No officers

110

in uniform — we don't want to spoil the day for these guys. But a lifer escaped from state prison last night and headed this way. We figure this would be a logical place for him to get dinner. Keep your own eyes peeled, will you, Sherlock?"

"But what does he look like?"

"That's the trouble — the description fits three-quarters of the men in here. Sixty, gray hair, undistinguished. Only picture was taken when he went in 30 years ago — not much help. Do your best. See you later." Tawson turned away.

Sara picked up the tray of turkey and carried it into the dining room. Chatting cheerfully as she served the first table, she paused for a moment to watch reactions to the fragrant food. Two men bowed their heads to say grace. One made the sign of the cross before lifting his fork. Another dropped his knife with a clatter, one dug into the turkey with his spoon, his neighbor sprinkled pepper until the bird was black. Several tucked napkins into their collars, and one, with a quick look around him, surreptitiously polished his silver on the edge of the tablecloth.

Sara waited until the men had nearly finished their dessert and coffee before she walked to the door and beckoned to a young officer in chinos and a baggy sweater. "Please be gentle," she said.

The policeman nodded and followed her back to the first table she had served. Sara indicated one of the gray-haired men.

"Mr. Bennett?" the officer asked quietly. The man's face flushed but, with a gesture of resignation, he stood up and held out his hands for the cuffs.

"I'm almost glad," he said. "Everything's changed too much — I couldn't get along outside. Thanks for the dinner, lady. But do you mind tellin' me — how did you spot me?"

What did Sara tell him?

Mr. Bennett had used a spoon to eat his turkey. In many prisons, a spoon is the only eating utensil provided, and just-released prisoners reach for it out of habit.

42 / THE BLONDE PRODUCER

From the crown of her broad-brimmed hat to the soles of her open-toed sandals, the big, blonde woman sent out waves of self-confidence. Little Mr. Bradkins, chairman of the town's library committee, beamed as he trotted into the library at her elbow.

"We have a very unusual opportunity here," he told Sara Hull. "Ever since the school board — of which, as you know, I am also a member — turned down the idea of a course in TV techniques because we had no one to teach it, we've had more and more requests for it from parents and students. Well, Miss Vandergroot here has offered to teach a TV course here this summer — and I thought we could make a room available for her right here in the library. She's asked for quite a high stipend but she's been a successful TV actress and producer in South Africa for the past ten years, and I think she's worth it."

"Have you checked Miss Vandergroot's credentials?" Sara asked.

The big woman's eyebrows went up, and Mr. Bradkins looked hurt.

"If you mean, have I written to Johannesburg, no, not yet," he said. "But she's told me all about her work — and here's a list of all the fine productions she's been associated with." He pulled out a handsomely printed two-page resumé. Sara took it and glanced at the descriptions of TV shows.

"Miss Vandergroot has a great deal of confidence," she said, "and that's the game she's playing with you, Mr. Bradkins. She has never worked in TV in South Africa."

How did Sara know?

It was simple. There is no television in the Union of South Africa.

43 / THE ZEPHYR

It was a glittering party. Women in expensive evening dresses set off by sparkling jewels, men dramatic in black and white contrasted with the gold-gleaming saris of Indian women, the vivid tribal dress of Africans, the flashing colors of military uniforms of a dozen countries. Sara Hull looked down at her plain dark-green evening dress and sighed. "Well," she said to Bill Tawson, "at least I don't have to worry about the Zephyr. He certainly won't go after my twenty-dollar pearls."

"Just keep your eyes and ears open," the detective inspector said. "Though what you're looking and listening for, nobody knows. The man is a great actor and a master at dialects and disguises. That's how he's managed to get away with four or five million dollars worth of jewelry during his career. He could be anybody, male or female, guest or servant." Sara sighed again.

"I'll mingle," she said, "but it's hardly the job for a librarian."

Moving from group to group, Sara caught snatches of intriguing conversation: "The Bangladesh problem has a simple solution, as I keep telling Indira Ghandi," a tall Sikh in a green turban told an equally tall, masculine-looking woman in what seemed to be a Chinese laborer's blouse and pants. "Yes, it was a souvenir of His Majesty King Edward the Eighth's coronation," said a long-faced Englishman, smiling down his high nose and holding out a diamond-studded watch fob to a dithering little American woman. "Her Serene Highness the Princess Anne used to play with it when she was a baby." "No one really understands the Kennedys," said a sleek-haired, effeminate-looking man, and his companion, a tall woman in silver, nodded. "She told me the same thing when I was at Hyannis last summer," she said. "But I've always thought Ari was a good sort, and Jackie too." A dark girl in gray chiffon buttonholed a bony little man with a French Legion d'Honneur button in his lapel and began, "Let me tell you about Rainier and Grace's latest — I saw it when I was in Monaco only last week, and you'll never believe — "

Sara caught Bill's eye, and they moved toward each other through the crowd. "Don't let that one leave," she whispered as they met, nodding almost imperceptibly toward one of the guests who was moving toward the door. Bill slipped away to alert his men. Only five minutes later the tall woman in silver let out a shriek. "My diamond earrings," she cried. "They're gone!"

Bill Tawson appeared in the doorway, held up his hands for quiet. "Please, ladies and gentlemen, everything is under control. The thief has been caught, and the earrings — and other jewels not yet missed — were found in his pocket. He is, by the way, the famous Zephyr, but he made a slip that tipped off — " he smiled toward Sara " — one of our agents."

How did Sara spot the thief?

The tall Englishman referred to Edward the Eighth's coronation and Her Serene Highness the Princess Anne. Edward VIII, later the Duke of Windsor, was never crowned. And British royalty does not use the designation "Serene Highness," but "Royal Highness."

44 / THE AGED
NEIGHBOR

"Miss Hull! Miss Hull!" Sara pushed away her coffee cup as her doorbell rang repeatedly and a frightened voice called her name. She opened the door to see her pretty young neighbor, Jane Barkley, crying hysterically.

"Oh, please come upstairs," Jane wailed, clutching at Sara's arm. "It's Aunt Lucie — I think she's dead!"

Together the two women ran up the short flight of stairs to Miss Lucie Barkley's one-room apartment, which was directly over her great-niece's. The door was open. Old Miss Barkley sat on the studio couch which served as her bed and sofa. In front of her was a small table on which stood a tray holding the remains of a half-eaten breakfast of steak and eggs. But the aged woman's head hung down, and blood flowed from a wound in her neck.

"Quick, a mirror!" Sara commanded. Jane fumbled through the clutter on top of a dresser, found a hand mirror, which Sara held up to the old woman's deeply sunken mouth. No mist formed.

"Yes, she *is* dead," Sara told the weeping girl. "Where's the phone? I'll call my friend Bill Tawson — he's a police inspector." As she placed the call, Sara looked around the crowded room. It was a den — a lair — filled with fussy necessities and the kind of precious junk a lonely old woman collects in more than eighty years of life. Medicine bottles were clustered on the dresser, false teeth floated in a glass of water on a bedside table, pincushions bristling with jewel-topped hatpins adorned the radiator top, hatboxes were stacked on chairs, the eyes of an old, fox-faced fur piece winked from a hat rack at pictures of babies in old-fashioned clothes smiling from gold and silver frames set up on every flat surface. Nostalgic tears were beginning to fill Sara's own eyes when Bill's voice interrupted her meditation on possessions and mortality. Waiting for him to come, Jane told Sara the story.

"Ever since I came to live here to be near Aunt Lucie, I've cooked breakfast for her in my apartment and brought it up here for her. This morning she started to eat, said how good the steak was, when I heard the phone ringing downstairs. I ran down — it was kind of a long call, and then

I straightened up my own room and came up for the dishes. The door was open — and she was sitting there, just the way she is. Somebody must have — " The doorbell rang, and Bill Tawson and two plainclothesmen came into the room. As the men busied themselves, Jane told her story again. Bill looked at Sara.

"Yes, Bill," Sara said, "I think you know. I'm sorry, Jane, but what you say can't be true. Now, did you eat half of that breakfast before you killed your aunt — or after?"

What did Sara mean?

night before.
glass where she had presumably placed them the
out teeth — and her false teeth were still in the
Miss Barkley could not have eaten steak with-

45 / THE VOICE OF
SUSANNA MARTIN

"I am Susanna Martin — Susanna Martin of Salem, Massachusetts!"

The big man's face was glossed with perspiration, his eyes fixed unseeingly on space. But what made Sara Hull's scalp tingle, in spite of the skepticism she had brought to this "seance," was the woman's voice that came out of his thin-lipped mouth. Ten minutes before, when he had smiled at the audience, leaned back in his armchair, and gone into his "trance state," he had spoken in a deep baritone, with an accent that seemed to have originated in the South. Now the voice was a sultry contralto, the accent that of New England. Gloria Bonney gasped and nudged Sara as the man's speech altered.

"See," she said, "it's just the way I said it

would be." Sara nodded. That afternoon, in the library where she worked for Sara after school, Gloria's plain, pleasant face had been pink with excitement as she described the previous meeting she had attended. "He can call back the spirit of this witch, who was executed in Salem back in 1692 — or 1693," she had explained. "And then, if you pay him twenty-five dollars, the witch will tell you how to make anything you want to happen." Gloria had looked wistful as she added, "Miss Hull, if Barney doesn't at least show that he notices me soon, I'll — well — "

Sara had understood. "Gloria," she had said, "witchcraft is an old religion and many very fine, intelligent people believe in it. But I've never heard of a witch being called back that way — and even if she was, I don't think she'd need money in the spirit world."

"But the things she tells people are true," Gloria had insisted. "Come and see." Sara had come, and was seeing.

"They were hard-faced men in black and gray," the woman's voice hissed out of the big man's mouth. "They found a mark on me that convinced them, and they sentenced me to die. Salem, Salem, I weep for you still. But then I screamed in agony as the flames crackled around me, charring my flesh, blistering my lips, loosening the flesh on my bones. I watched my hands burn from my wrists — all my spells were not strong enough to stop the pain. But I have learned more in the other world since then — "

Sara Hull took Gloria firmly by the hand, and

propelled her out into the hall, as the girl protested. "I want to go back — how can you doubt her — can't you feel the fire? It had to be real — "

"Gloria," Sara said, "that man is very clever in disguising his voice. I don't say he can't contact the dead — I don't know. But I do know that the voice of Susanna Martin is a fraud, and I can prove it."

How could Sara prove it?

With any encyclopedia. In Salem, Massachusetts, during the witch hunt of the seventeenth century, supposed witches were hanged and one was pressed to death with stones. But no witches were ever burned in Salem.

46 / THE ANCIENT AARDVARK

The Larrington mansion gleamed white in the twilight as Sara Hull and Bill Tawson mounted the steps between the great pillars and rang the bell. The door was opened almost instantly, not by one of the servants, but by young Tom Larrington himself. A look of surprise crossed his weak, pleasant face when he saw the librarian and the detective. Then he threw the door open wide.

"Come in, Miss Hull, and Inspector Tawson, this is a pleasure. Not an official call, I trust?"

"No, Sara had some crossword puzzle books for your great-uncle, and I thought I'd look in on the old gentleman too. Haven't seen him since he's been bedridden."

"Oh, good," said Tom, "right up here," and the

three began to climb the sweeping stairway that rose from the tile-floored hall. "He needs company. He's been depressed lately. Sits and types the names of departed friends on his portable typewriter, then moans that he's the last of his kind. Except for that, crossword puzzles are his only activity."

"Well, he's good at them," Sara said. They had reached the second floor, and Tom knocked discreetly on a closed door. There was no answer. He banged harder. Still no sound.

"Oh, dear, he must have dropped off to sleep," Tom said. "Well, we'll just have to wake him up — he'd never forgive me if you left without seeing him. He has plenty of time for naps." He turned the doorknob and went into the bedroom, followed by Sara and Bill. "Oh, no," Tom gasped.

Old Horace Larrington lay halfway out of a bed splattered with blood, a gaping hole in his head. Near his dangling hand lay a pistol.

"I shouldn't have left him when he was so depressed," Tom wailed. "Look, the poor old dear left a note." He picked up a typed sheet of paper from the bed and read aloud:

"My species will soon be extinct, like the platypus and the aardvark. I do not want to wait any longer. All I have is yours, dear nephew — use it well. Horace Larrington." Tom dropped the paper and buried his face in his hands. Sara picked up the note.

Frowning, she reread it silently, then looked hard at Tom Larrington's bent head.

"Bill," she said, "don't call the suicide squad.

Horace Larrington didn't type this note. I think you've got a murder on your hands."

How did Sara know?

A crossword puzzle enthusiast like Horace would have known that the platypus and aardvark, animals often mentioned in puzzles, are not extinct, but very much alive in Australia and South Africa, respectively.

47 / THE FURIOUS FARMER

"Next time I give a speech to a 4-H Club out in the country I'll be sure I have a spare tire," Bill Tawson grumbled. "Do you know it's nearly two A.M.? It took that mechanic nearly three hours — "

"But it's a beautiful night for a drive in the country air." Sara Hull rested her head on Bill's shoulder. "Your speech was — hey, look!" The headlights showed a young man in overalls standing in the middle of the road waving his arms.

"Will you take me to a police station?" the young man cried, rushing over to the window as Bill slowed down. "My father has been slugged, and our phone's out of order and my car won't start — "

"At your service," Bill said, showing his detective inspector's badge and patting his gun. "Get in."

127

On the way up the lane to the farmhouse the young farmer explained.

"My brother and his wife sleep in the room next to Dad's, but it's hard to wake them up. Edna finally did hear something, though, and got Matt up. He ran in and there was Dad on the floor, out cold, with a big bruise on his chin. The bed was all torn apart, and the bureau drawers had been gone through. We've locked the doors so nobody can leave — we've got three tourists spending the night here, but only one is up. He said he didn't hear anything, but he was standing by his window and saw a man running across the yard. The others are women — "

In the big farmhouse kitchen a husky young farmer and his pretty wife hovered over a silver-haired, elderly man in pajamas, holding an ice bag to his chin. Nearby stood a tall, broad-shouldered man in a maroon dressing gown, smoking an aluminum pipe.

"I was in my room down the hall when it must have happened. I was awake, looking out the window," he continued, after telling Bill his name was Ralph Warrox. "I couldn't sleep — how can anybody say the country is quiet? All those birds flying around, and cows mooing in the fields or barn or wherever they keep them, and dogs barking, and roosters crowing, and chickens cackling, and horses neighing, and tree branches hitting the house. A sleeping pill salesman could make a fortune! Anyway, that's why I was up and at the window. I saw a man running away from the house, across the barnyard. He stumbled over some of the chickens asleep on the ground, but he went on out over the fields — and just about that time I heard all the commotion in my host's room."

Sara Hull laughed out loud, and the farm family joined her.

"Mr. Warrox," she said, "next time you plan a robbery in the country, you'd better think it over. I doubt that many farmers keep their money in mattresses any more. And, in addition — "

What did Sara add?

"Nobody ever stumbled over a chicken asleep on the ground. And anybody who heard chickens cackling and other birds flying and roosters crowing before two A.M. had something else on his mind. Birds roost — sleep on perches or in trees — from sundown to sunup, which may seem early to city people, but isn't THAT early."

48 / THE BOY
WHO FORETOLD
THE FUTURE

"Yeah, I need an after-school job," the tall, muscular teenager told Sara. "I could lift boxes of books or something — I'm strong. Not much good at desk work, though."

"Have you worked before?" Sara asked.

"Yeah, but the guy got scared because — well, you look like the kind of old lady I can tell. I got this kind of — like a gift, see? I dream stuff and it comes true. Well, I usedta work nights in Glixon's Garage — I'm old enough, and I'm big enough to be a good night watchman. Just keep an eye out, don't let nobody come in, that kind of stuff. Well, this night I have a dream that old Glixon is gonna fall down a flight of stairs. He's not a bad guy, and I know what I dream that way comes true. So, I go to the phone and call his house and ask for him and his old lady is real uptight and tells me he can't come to the phone because — you guessed it — he hadda go to the doctor because he fell down the cellar stairs. Well, naturally, I told her that I'd called to warn him about that, and that I was sorry I didn't get to the phone on time. She was real nice, but you know what? The next day old Glixon comes hobblin' in on crutches, and fires me! It wasn't my fault I didn't let him know on time — I did the best I could —"

"Did you really?" Sara said. "I'm sorry, but I don't think you'd fit in here too well, either. I'm not prejudiced against people who have psychic experiences. You might even be very valuable to us that way. But until there's a budget for library assistants who foretell the future, I'm afraid we'll have to stick with hiring people we can trust."

Why didn't Sara trust the teenager?

To dream that his boss was going to fall down-stairs, the night watchman had to be sleeping on the job — not a very good recommendation.

49 / THE FAMOUS AUTHOR

"Are you the librarian in charge?" The man was tall, gray-bearded, with an air of both sensitivity and confidence. Sara Hull acknowledged her position, and he leaned close to her. "Is there somewhere we could — speak privately?"

"Why, yes, I have an office right over here." Sara led him to her office, closed the door, and indicated a chair.

"This is very embarrassing," the man said. "I don't suppose you recognize me — perhaps from seeing my picture, perhaps from the lecture platform — no? Well, I'm Pervis Clement Way."

"Oh!" Sara was impressed by the name of the famous novelist. "This is an honor, Mr. Way. But — you said your business was embarrassing — ?"

"I'm afraid it is, rather. I hardly know where to

132

begin. I was on my way to New York, and when the train stopped here I remembered an old friend who lives in this town — someone I haven't seen in years. Stuart Woffington — " It was the name of one of the town's most prominent citizens. "Well, just on impulse I decided to get off that train and go over and see Stu. I got off all right, went into a phone booth to call him — and found I didn't have a cent. My wallet was gone — all my money, credit cards, everything. Couldn't even make the call. Well, I walked out of the station not knowing what to do. Just walked for a few minutes, until I saw the library. 'Way,' I said to myself, 'they'll know you there if they do anywhere.' I came in, and — here I am."

"Shall I call Mr. Woffington for you?" Sara offered, and then remembered. "Oh, dear, Mr. Way, I'm afraid I can't do that. The Woffingtons are in Europe — I remember reading that they'd left in last Sunday's society pages. Do you know anyone else in town?"

"No one I can think of. Miss Hull, I assure you that I can be trusted. Could you — yourself — twenty-five dollars perhaps? I'll write you an IOU and send you my personal check the moment I get back to my apartment in New York." Sara hesitated, and Way turned on his charm. "Look, if you've any doubt about me — there's identification right over there on your shelves. My photograph is on the back of every dust jacket of every one of my books. I assume you cover the jackets with those plastic covers? Well, I'm a profligate author, as you know, so you must

133

have a dozen or so pictures of me within a few feet. Don't think I'll be insulted — please, look me up."

"I don't really have to, Mr. — not Mr. Way," Sara said, rising. "I'm sure there's a picture of a bearded man who looks something like you on every one of those book covers. But it's not your picture. You've probably done this quite a few times before. The gentleman behind you — you can see him through the glass panel there, just outside the door — will be able to tell us. He's Detective Inspector Bill Tawson, coming to take me to lunch. But I'm not very hungry. I'd much rather help catch an impostor and confidence man."

What gave "Way" away?

Look up the meaning of the word "profligate." Hardly a mistake a man of letters would make in describing himself, true though it might have been. "Way," meant to say he was a "prolific" author, meaning he'd written a lot of books.

50 / SCATTERBRAINED CINDY

"Cindy," Sara Hull said to her young library assistant, "this book is reserved for Dr. Henry Marek. He's coming back for it precisely at six and he's in a big hurry, so if I'm not right here, give it to him."

"Sure," said Cindy, shifting her chewing gum as she scribbled a name on a slip of paper and stuck it in the book. Sara caught a glimpse of the name, in Cindy's careless scrawl: Dr. Jimmy Marek. She sighed. In the two weeks since she had been working here, Cindy had grown more and more incapable of getting anything right. Now she was on the phone again, making one of her loud, endless personal phone calls about boys and dates. "Well, at least I can fire her without hurting her feelings," Sara thought. "I told her when she came that we needed someone with a smattering of French and German, and she doesn't know any language but English."

At six Sara was in the stacks. A few seconds later she heard a sound outside the building that sounded like a car backfiring repeatedly. But screams convinced her that it was gunfire. Running to the door, she saw Dr. Henry Marek sprawled on the steps, blood from many wounds staining the white marble. Police were already scrambling toward the body, and within minutes Bill Tawson had arrived and was questioning the frightened staff and the few readers who had been in the library when Marek entered, left, and died.

"We're not really surprised at this," he said. "Marek had been involved in the Czech underground, and he had enemies. But he knew it, and never told anyone — ever — where he was going or what he planned to do. Yet somebody knew he would come out of the library at that particular moment. The rookie on the beat across the street said a gray car pulled up just as Marek made a perfect target on the steps. A man in the front seat did the job, and the car speeded away. The question is: Who tipped them off?"

Sara Hull's eyes widened. "Cindy!" she said. "You could have done it easily. You've known for hours that Marek — "

"What do you mean?" Cindy cried. "I didn't even know him — why would I — "

"I don't know," Sara said coldly. "But there's something you do know — though you told me

136

When told the book was for a man named Henry, Cindy wrote what looked like "Jimmy" to Sara — until Sara remembered that, in Czech, Henry is written as *Jimry*.

How did Sara know?

you only knew English. You know the Czech language!"

51 / THE DICKENS LETTER

"Sara, couldn't you get some help from a home for senior citizens?" Mr. Branning was always crotchety when he was setting up a new exhibit, but Sara sighed and listened. "Those young people! That Marty, who's supposed to be cleaning the cases for the Dickens exhibit — away for a cigarette every ten minutes! That Jessie keeps dropping the folders, and that Andrea! First she combs her hair over the case where she's supposed to be helping me arrange books and letters, then she stops to put on nail polish. I thought kids didn't use cosmetics any more! Lipstick too — she puts more on every five minutes! We'll be forever!" And he stormed back to the exhibit hall to harrass his young assistants a while longer.

In spite of their shortcomings, the young people under Mr. Branning's supervision had the Dickens exhibit ready for the public by early afternoon. It proved instantly popular. People streamed past the cases, pointing to favorite passages in Dickens' own writing, exclaiming over the withered flower from his buttonhole. "My mother saw him on the stage when he was in New York," an old man in spats and white gloves confided to Sara. And an elderly woman with an arm in a sling was wet-eyed when she said, "The death of Little Nell is the saddest story in the world."

But it all stopped at four o'clock when Mr. Branning ran into the main reading room, ignoring the silence signs to scream, "Dickens' letter to his sister-in-law! It's gone! Somebody cut a hole in the case and took it! Oh, it's worth a small fortune, it's priceless, it's irreplaceable — "

"It's going to be hard to run this down," the detective assigned to the theft admitted. "Dozens of people had a chance to do it, and it could be sold to a private collector and disappear for years. But, to begin, we'll have to fingerprint everyone on your staff so we'll know which prints we *won't* have to check out."

Obediently, the librarians lined up to have their fingers inked, some willing, others protesting. Later, driving to a film with Detective Inspector Bill Tawson, Sara inquired about possible progress.

"None," Bill reported glumly. "It'll be like finding a needle in a haystack. So far, the only prints on the case we recognize are Branning's, and,

though we're checking him out, he seems an un-
likely suspect."

Sara sat up straight. "I know who did it," she
said.

Do you know?

It was Andrea. By painting nail polish on her
fingertips, she masked her fingerprints — for-
getting that they SHOULD be on a case in which
she'd arranged an exhibit.

52 / "ALAS!" CRIED YORICK

Barrymore Yorick, retired actor, strode grandly into the library every morning at a few minutes past nine. "Walk a mile, ends right here," he explained to Sara, but she knew that reading one of the morning papers she put out saved a dime from a meager pension. Rolf Marver arrived every day a few minutes later, also pink from a mile's walk from the opposite direction, and for just the same reason. But Rolf had millions — saving dimes in ways like this helped him hang onto them. Barrymore and Rolf detested each other, and always sat opposite each other at the round table near the paper and magazine rack, holding the newspapers open in front of their faces to avoid each other's eyes. Today, between them, also behind a spread paper, sat a tall tourist from the Crown Hotel, absorbing some news before her sightseeing bus pulled up across the street. Several other tourists, killing time for the same purpose, stood at the rack fingering magazines, or absently flicked the pages of books from nearby shelves.

But nobody went sightseeing that morning. At nine-ten, old Rolf Marver's chair tilted back and he crashed, in it, to the floor. Librarians and readers rushed to him — to find a knife still protruding from between his shoulder blades. "Alas!" Barrymore Yorick cried, striking his breast. "He was mine enemy but I would not have wished him this!"

Detective Inspector Bill Tawson, a little later, didn't seem quite so sure. "You say, Mr. Yorick, that you had just begun to read the paper when Mr. Marver fell. What were you reading?"

"Why, the theater review," Barrymore answered. "And what did it say?" Bill asked, nodding to Sara, who quietly took one of the newspapers left in the rack and opened it to the theater page.

"The reviewer felt that the King Lear was mediocre, but remarked at the end that Cordelia had a future in — let's see — 'turning priggish princesses into sympathetic princesses.' " Sara nodded back to Bill — the quote was exact.

"And what were you doing a few minutes before the crash?" Bill asked a beautiful black tourist. "Well, it's — I'm a model and my picture was supposed to be in the new *Vogue*," the girl explained modestly. "It just came out yesterday, and I was looking — " Sara found the girl's picture, glamorous in a gold jump suit, in a maga-

142

zine that had been hastily stuffed, open, back into the rack.

"And you?" The tall tourist who had sat at the table pulled at a button of her wine-colored suit as she said, "I was looking up my horoscope. That's why I came in — I didn't want to carry a paper all day, but I do have to know what the stars say — "

"What's your sign?" Sara asked, turning to the page.

"Why, I'm a Uranus — I'm supposed to have a — well, a kind of mixed day, watch out for other people — " Sara checked the column.

"I was just killing — oh! — I mean, trying to fill in time," a leathery-faced man in a blue suit said. "I was looking at a book of old short stories from one of those shelves. It was O. Henry's thing about the Magi — the girl with the hair — I was reading when I heard — " Sara found the book on top of other books on the fiction shelf.

Bill looked into her eyes and seemed to read a message.

"I think we can stop this line of questioning right now," he said. "I want all of you to stay here for a while, but I'm afraid you — " he pointed " — will have to answer a few more questions."

Which reader did Bill point to?

The tall tourist in the red suit, who turned out to be an heir Marvel didn't know. Uranus is not one of the twelve signs of the zodiac.

53 / THE DRUG DEALER

"You think I'm prejudiced against Pat because she's black, don't you?"

Sara Hull looked squarely into Jean McCabe's blue eyes.

"Yes, I do think so," she said frankly. "Ever since you both came here to work after school you've done nothing but criticize Pat, though she's an excellent worker. She's tried to be friendly to you, and you've been cold and distant."

"I've been cold because I didn't trust her," Jean said, her face reddening. "And now I know I was right. She's in trouble, Miss Hull, just as I thought she'd be sooner or later. Haven't you ever noticed? Whenever she's working here at five o'clock, she goes over to the encyclopedia shelf and takes down Volume X or Y of the Encyclopaedia Britannica, and pretends to look something up. If one of the volumes is out of order, she puts them in order, very carefully. Then she leaves and in just a few seconds a big black kid in a leather jacket comes in and does the same thing — takes down either the X or the Y volume. Well, yesterday I got close enough to Pat to see what it was all about. She put this between the X and Y volumes. Boy, was that kid surprised when he didn't find it!" She held out a tiny glassine envelope filled with white powder. "I'll bet he takes it and leaves money for her — that way they never seem to speak to each other, but the stuff gets delivered."

Sara looked shocked. "Heroin?" she said.

"I don't know," Jean answered, "how could I? I don't do drugs. Shall I call the police, Miss Hull? Or do you want to do it?"

"If you really believe there's heroin in that envelope, you'll have to go to the police and explain where you got it," Sara said. "I should really let you go and tell the story you've just told me so you'll find out that lying doesn't pay. Pat didn't put that envelope where you say she did, and you didn't find it there. And if you spread that story around, I'll be right there to expose it for the malicious falsehood it is."

How could Sara be so sure?

Encyclopedias like the Britannica don't have a volume for each letter — and entries beginning with X, Y, and Z are invariably in the same volume.

54 / THE THREATENED PROFESSOR

"I'll take you to Randall Wood Roddinger's lecture," Bill Tawson said, "but I'll be on duty. The professor has really stirred up some activists who don't share his point of view, and there's been a kidnap threat. We've got to watch him every minute he's not onstage."

"I didn't really expect you to pay much attention to me while the leading authority on American history in the world is speaking," Sara said. And she was careful not to make comments to Bill during the professor's reading of a masterly comparison of America in the nineteenth and twentieth centuries.

At the end of the talk a young man rose to ask a question.

"Professor Roddinger," he addressed the thin, hawk-nosed man in gray, "I'm Alex Birk, majoring in American history at the University. In your last book you said, if I quote you correctly, that the eight years of Grover Cleveland's administration were 'eight unbroken years of poverty and trouble, relieved by such distractions as the President's marriage and the dedication of the Statue of Liberty.'" Roddinger smiled, nodding assent. "Well, I disagree," the young man went on. "You're blaming Cleveland for almost a decade of disturbance. Personally, I think those eight years were among the most comfortable for the average citizen, simply because none of his values were being challenged. I think — " Hands were waving wildly all over the hall, but Roddinger ignored them, listening closely to the young student. Sara poked Bill's arm, hard.

"Bill, get out of here and find the real professor," she gasped. "That man's a double; and send somebody to arrest that student — he's in on the kidnap plot!"

The professor was found in a speeding car, bound and gagged, already almost fifty miles away. Roddinger was revealed as a clever impersonator, and the "student" a member of the activist group. The speech, cleverly based on Roddinger's books, and the lengthy "question" were staged to gain time for their accomplices' getaway with the real Dr. Roddinger.

How did Sara know?

A historian, and a student of history, would both have known that Cleveland didn't serve "eight unbroken years." He was defeated in the election of 1888 after one term, and reelected in 1892 — the only President that ever happened to.

55 / THE MIGHTY HUNTER

"Honestly, some people are such hypocrites it makes you sick!" Joanne Watson's eyes flashed with anger as she slammed a book down on the library desk. "Miss Hull, what do you think of a senior who has campaigned all over the community against hunting, and then goes out and shoots two deer — and out of season, at that?"

"Are you talking about Lewis Grant?" Sara was incredulous, but Joanne nodded. "I find that almost impossible to believe. Why, Lewis was even cited for his fine work by the National Animal Protection League. Are you sure he went hunting?"

"I heard him say it himself. His locker is near mine, and I heard him tell Rod Bradburk that the animals had been driving his mother crazy. They live in that house on the edge of the woods, you know, and he's always said how he loved to watch the deer. Anyway, he said he didn't blame his mother, and he did away with a buck and a doe, which might help for a while."

"A doe! But no one is allowed to shoot female deer in this state — even *in* hunting season!"

"I know. What do you think I ought to do, Miss Hull? Call the game warden? At least I'm going to call a special meeting of the Ecology Club, and demand Lewis's resignation."

Sara was equally appalled. "When I think of Lewis Grant taking a gun and shooting deer — " she stopped short. "Joanne, did he say he shot them?"

"No, I didn't actually hear him say he used a gun. But how else would you kill deer? Honestly — "

"Joanne, I want you to promise me something," Sara interrupted. "Before you do anything about this, or even talk to anyone else about it, will you find Lewis, tell him what you overheard, and ask him to explain it? I believe he did just what you heard him say he did, but I think you should hear him say it to your face."

Next afternoon, Lewis and Joanne came into the library hand-in-hand.

"Yes," Joanne smiled at Sara, "he killed them, all right. But I think even the Animal Protection League will understand."

Why was Lewis' action acceptable?

The buck and doe were rats. Not only deer, but rats, mice, rabbits, and goats are called bucks and does.

56 / THE CRAZY CROWD

Prisca Pippin's famous freckles stood out like dots of rust on her chalk-white face. Her green eyes did not need the stage makeup that made them look wide and frightened. "I can't believe it," she kept saying, "I can't believe it. Who'd want to murder Eddie?"

But someone had wanted to murder Eddie Looden, Prisca's partner in the zany "Crazy Crowd" dance they had performed for cheering audiences all over the world. Someone, in the course of the wild mob scene, had brushed against Eddie and stabbed him. But who? Prisca wouldn't believe that it was one of the members of her troupe. "They loved Eddie," she said. "He was the sweetest guy in the world." And all the dancers, sitting now in the two front rows of the theater with Bill Tawson standing in front of them like a stern teacher, agreed. Sara Hull, who had been in the audience when the crime took place, sat in a side seat.

"You know all these people?" Bill asked Prisca, indicating the three rows of dancers. "Well, most of them," Prisca answered the detective inspector. "But not all. Some of the regulars couldn't make this tour, and my agent hired some new people in New York just before we left. He didn't come with us tonight, and some of the new dancers didn't come with us on the plane, either, just reported at rehearsal. The 'Crazy Crowd' dance isn't carefully choreographed, you see. Any good professional — or even a talented amateur — can learn it quickly."

"You mean some of these people may not even be on the payroll?"

"Oh, I don't think anyone just did the show for fun," Prisca said, but her expression was a little doubtful.

"Well, I'm going to have to ask all of you just where you were when Mr. Looden was killed," Bill told the dancers. "I'll start with you." He pointed to a tall girl, who said, "I was right over there near the door," and she indicated the polka-dot door onstage that was one of the features of the "Crazy Crowd" scene.

"I was there by the fireplug," said a dancer in a dog suit, but for once no one laughed.

"I was jumping up and down on the park bench downstage," a girl in a pink hair bow said.

A man in a windowpane checked suit and a wildly striped tie explained, "I was there at stage

151

right, near the purple piano," and he pointed to the right of the stage.

"I was at center stage, passing in front of Eddie, with my back to him," a thin girl dressed like a skeleton said. Sara Hull stood up, went over to Bill, and drew him aside.

"I think I know which one of them isn't a professional," she said softly.

Which dancer did Sara name?

The man in the windowpane checks, who turned out to be a mental patient who imagined Eddie had harmed him. A professional performer would have known that stage right is the actor's right, what the audience would describe as left.

57 | A TALE OF TIME AND THYME

"Strom Thyme was alive and well when I left him at eleven last night!" Kroll Bolling insisted. Thyme's next-door neighbor, Mrs. Quency, agreed. "I was just coming home, and my grandfather clock was chiming eleven as I opened my door," she said. "I know Mr. Bolling, he often has dinner in Mr. Thyme's apartment — Mr. Thyme loves to cook. Mr. Bolling called back, 'That's all right, Strom, I'll let myself out,' nodded to me, and went down the stairs. The doors lock behind us here — no, I didn't hear another sound from Mr. Thyme's side of the wall all night."

"I came to work at about five minutes to twelve," said Minna Canny, Thyme's housekeeper, wiping away a tear. "I'd stopped at the store, and the delivery boy came back with me to carry the groceries. I let myself in — I have a key — the boy set the box down in the kitchen — and Mr. Thyme's clock radio went off in his bedroom. It was loud, we both heard it. By then — yes, it was about a minute after noon — the whistle had blown just as we came in, and the radio started as it died away. It's a new clock radio, one of those — digital, is it? — things, no hands. The boy left, I went to work in the kitchen — there were two cups, two plates, Mr. Thyme had had Mr. Bolling to dinner again. The radio stopped playing in about an hour, and I thought Mr. Thyme would come out to eat, but he didn't. About two o'clock, the phone rang. I answered it — it was for Mr. Thyme, of course, and I went and knocked on his bedroom door. No answer. I banged, then pushed it open — all that blood — "

"The press is right — Minna gave Bolling a perfect alibi," Bill Tawson told Sara Hull. "The delivery boy confirms the time the clock radio began to play. The coroner says Thyme died between ten thirty last night and a little after midnight. And it's obvious that someone had to be alive in Thyme's apartment after midnight. Why? Sara! Because, if the clock had been set for twelve, it would have gone off at midnight, played for awhile, turned itself off automatically, as Minna didn't know it could. But it couldn't have reset itself for noon — so somebody had to set it after midnight. It's a classic clue, and it gives Bolling a clean bill. Minna spent the night with her little boy in the hospital — tonsils — she's clear. So — "

"Bill, I'm surprised at you," Sara said. "Thyme

himself, or even Bolling could have set that clock radio long before midnight."

How could an alarm clock set for twelve not go off for more than 12 hours?

A digital clock radio, unlike a regular clock, has two 12s — it must be set for either A.M. or P.M. — 12 noon or 12 midnight. Bolling was the killer.

58 / THE MAN IN THE GREEN TURBAN

"Excuse me, please." Under the carefully wound green turban, the tall man's face was like a fine wood carving. His English was precise but strongly accented as he explained: "I am one of a group of Indian students at the University who have been receiving very sad letters from home about a sorrowful plague that has hit our native province. I know that you cannot let me move among the readers here in your library to ask for funds, but I wonder if I might be allowed to leave one of our receptacles in a prominent place, so that kind Americans might drop coins — or dollars — into it to help my unhappy countrymen."

He held out a round can with a slit in the top, and a label showing a weeping Indian child. "Rancipur Relief Fund," it read and, in smaller print: "Please help the victims of the python plague that is sweeping Rancipur. Snakes from the jungles are invading the villages, and their venom is causing terrible illness and death. Funds are needed for medicines and hospital care. Please give generously."

Sara shook her head. "This is really terrible —"

"Ah, yes," said the tall man, breaking in. "If you had ever seen a child bitten by a python — "

"I am sure I would be shocked. Just as I am by this fraud. Now, take your receptacle and go — while I call the Bureau of Consumer Protection and report you for trying to get money under false pretenses!" The man gasped and hurried from the library, as Sara picked up the phone.

How did she know his "charity" was a fraud?

Pythons don't bite — they can kill, but it's by squeezing their victims to death.

59 / UNCLE XAVIER

Amanda Hull had died at ninety, still full of zest for life. She had been smiling, her nephew Xavier Hull reported, when he found her lying beside her favorite chair. Apparently a stroke had felled her as she was about to write a cheerful note to one of her relatives, for her rosewood writing desk lay overturned beside her. There was a bump on her temple, but even the doctor agreed that it had been made when, falling, she hit her head on the corner of a table.

Sara, only a distant cousin, had always admired the old lady and had been glad she was not involved in the constant squabbling among her heirs. The only one she sincerely liked was young Alice Hull, who now stood in Amanda's living room, tearfully holding out a piece of paper.

"Cousin Sara, I called you because I don't know what to think. Look, this note is in Grandma's writing. I found it under the big chair Uncle Xavier said she must have been sitting in when she fell. You know how rich he is, and how he's

158

always fighting with everybody over money, and saying Grandma had a lot of money stashed away and he wanted his share. Well, just read it. I don't really like Uncle Xavier, but I want to believe he just happened to drop by and find her, the way he says. But — that bump on her head — Maybe she knew he was coming and — or maybe she was afraid of him — "

Sara took the note and looked closely at the old woman's spidery handwriting:

"Alice, beware! Caution, don't ever forget! (Gold hidden in jar — keep looking.) My nephew owns plenty. Quarrelsome relatives sometimes tell untruths — vicious, wild. Xavier — " here the piece of paper was torn across, so the last words were lost.

"Do you think we should call the police?" Alice asked.

"No, I don't," Sara said. "It's a suspicious-sounding note, all right. But look at it carefully, Alice. Do you really think anybody who was really afraid would take the time to write a note like that? It explains why your grandmother was smiling — but I wouldn't count on finding any money in a jar, if I were you."

Why was Sara so sure?

Every word in the note is followed by one beginning with the next, consecutive letter of the alphabet — Alice, beware! Caution," etc. As Sara said, a seriously frightened old lady wouldn't have taken time to play a game like this.